PURSUIT OF MAGIC

DRAGON'S GIFT THE VALKYRIE BOOK 3

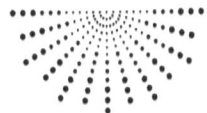

LINSEY HALL

For Jenn, a real Wonder Woman.

CHAPTER ONE

Grassmarket, Supernatural District of Edinburgh
Two days after the events in Academy of Magic

I crouched on the rooftop, the cool breeze blowing my hair away from my face. Three stories below, the Grassmarket was unusually silent for early afternoon.

Normally, the supernatural district of Edinburgh would be bustling. But today, tension crackled on the air and the street was empty.

A fight was about to go down, and anybody with half a brain was hiding out. Except me. Because I was here to start the fight.

"They'll be here any minute." Ana surveyed the cobblestone street.

"As long as the Protectorate's intel was correct," I murmured.

Yesterday, we'd received word that a mob boss had moved his operations from The Vault, the underground dark magic section of town, to the main street in the Grassmarket. Today, he was planning to send his goons to threaten the shopkeepers into turning over part of their profits.

As self-appointed guardian of the little guys, the Protectorate was stepping in to take care of business. And since I'd had enough of mob bosses, I was happy to join the team.

"Our first real life operation," Ana said. "And I'm so ready."

We were here as part of our training for the Academy. On the rooftop two buildings over, Lacey and Oscar, two other trainees, were waiting to do their part.

I scanned the street, searching for Cade, whom I hadn't seen since our kiss in the Whisky and Warlock two days ago. I spotted him, lurking in an alley near an enchanted bakery. Other Protectorate members hid out as well, in alleys and behind parked cars.

"There." Ana pointed down the street.

A fleet of big black SUVs drove down the cobblestone street.

"Why do mob bosses always like those cars?" I muttered.

"They think it makes them look badass," Ana said.

"Our buggy is badass. Those are meant for ferrying kids to Little League."

Ana chuckled. "Hey, that's a hard job."

"Actually, yeah. But the buggy is still cooler."

"Agreed." I crouched low on the roof so it would be hard to see me. If they looked carefully they would, but no need to borrow trouble.

The cars pulled to a stop on the main street, right in front of the most successful shops in the Grassmarket. This was where they'd start with their threats, which, according to our intel, usually involved injury for the shop owners.

We couldn't let that happen.

Especially not on our turf. This was our part of town. This job was personal.

Men and women piled out of the big cars, all of them dressed in black. Horns protruded from their heads, and they had fangs and crazy skin tones like ivory and red.

"Demons." Joy lit Ana's voice.

"Jackpot." We could kill demons without feeling guilty.

Sending them back to the Underworld was our duty. And privilege.

Demons were often hired by creeps and villains, taken out of the Underworld and used to commit atrocious deeds.

There were at least fifteen of them. I sucked in a breath, readying my magic.

In the alley below, Cade raised a fist.

The signal to start. As the most experienced fighter, he was the boss on this operation.

As one, the Protectorate members flowed out from alleyways, racing into the cobblestone street. There were six total—Cade, Jude, Caro, Ali, Haris, and Ammons, who ran the Demon Tracker Unit. They could handle the fifteen, as long as the fifteen were cornered. Trapped.

Which was my job.

I bounced lightly on my feet, waiting for my signal.

One of the mob demons shouted, pointing to the oncoming Protectorate members. As planned, the demons hadn't yet reached the sidewalk. They were still in the street.

As soon as our guys joined them, Cade raised his hand, two fingers pointed skyward.

My cue.

I hurled my magic outward, sending it toward the sewers beneath the street. It was my job to create a wall of water, trapping the demons in the street so the Protectorate could take them out. They'd never even make it into a shop to issue their ugly threats.

My friends charged the demons, who had started to go toward the shops to harass the owners. I envisioned the water in the sewers shooting out of the storm drains and forming a wall, trapping the fight in the street. I'd create a coliseum of water and cobblestone ground, with walls of water trapping the bad guys so that my friends could take them out.

But my magic faltered, weakening in my chest. Nausea rose

inside me. I pushed harder, begging my magic to work. I'd lost my sonic boom power, so I needed this.

"You can do it," Ana murmured.

Sweat dripped down my temple. My muscles ached and my head buzzed.

I sucked in a ragged breath, ignored the nausea, and pushed harder.

Finally, water shot from the storm drains, forming a wall around the fighters in the middle of the street. It cut off a group of three that were racing for a potions shop. Ali and Haris, the Djinns, sprinted toward them, disappearing into two of the demons, who began to fight each other. Ali and Haris would keep it up until the demons were almost dead, then they would jump out.

Behind them, Jude flicked an electric whip that sparkled like her starry eyes. It wrapped around a tall demon with massive red horns, snapping him in half.

I winced, bile rising in my throat.

"She means business," Ana murmured.

"Gotta be tough." And Jude was *super* tough.

Caro, her platinum hair glinting in the sun, shot her jet of deadly water at a blue demon who was bearing down on her with flaming hands. It pierced the demon's chest and flowed out the back as a red stream.

"Take that!" she yelled.

Cade, all lethal grace, hurled his silver shield toward two mages, beheading them in quick succession. The heads flew into the air as blood spurted.

The shield returned to Cade, and he caught it, ready to hurl again. He took aim for two more demons, but the trainees on the other building threw fireballs, taking them out first.

Cade grinned, then turned to another.

As if on cue, a demon looked up at us on the roof. Her black hair blew back from her horns, and she frowned, her fangs long and jagged.

"Yeah, it's me," I muttered. "I'm making the wall of water."

Though she couldn't hear me, she seemed to realize what was going on. If these bastards had any hope of surviving, much less threatening the shopkeepers they'd come to harass, they'd have to get by my wall.

She raised her hands, which glowed with yellow light.

"No idea what that is. But I want no part." Ana raised her hands, her magic swelling on the air, and produced a shield. The demon hurled her magic.

The magic slammed into Ana's shield and dissipated.

"Ha! Don't like that, do you?" Ana cackled.

The demon shrieked her rage.

In my chest, my magic faltered again. Queasiness made sweat break out on my skin. My grip on the water was fading. Before, I'd been able to feel the water in my chest—a deep knowing. Now, I felt only a trickle.

Sweating, I focused, putting all my attention toward keeping the wall of water high and strong. Beside me, Ana repelled the woman's attacks, keeping her blows from hitting me.

We'd always made a good team.

But my gift faltered again, the wall of water dropping by several feet as my control weakened.

We'd only make a good team if I could do my part.

"Come on, Bree," Ana muttered.

I struggled, giving it my all, but the wall of water continued to drop. *No, no, no.*

The fight was still raging in the street, but there were several demon mobsters trying to break through my water wall to get to the shop owners. Or hell, maybe they were just trying to escape Cade's deadly wrath.

Whatever the case, I was all that stood between them and escape.

And my chest was starting to feel empty, my stomach acidic. The wall of water continued to drop. Panic beat frantic wings inside my mind.

"Bree!" Ana said. "Get it together. They're going to escape. We need to send them back to hell."

"I know." I gasped, mind buzzing.

This was *so* bad.

Cade glanced up at me, concern creasing his brow.

Finally, the water crashed to the ground, my magic tapped out. I collapsed, barely catching myself with my hands.

Shit, shit, shit.

I shook my head, panting, and looked up. Ana still had her shield raised, but the demon woman had stopped attacking. She was running for the shops, instead.

"We've got to fight," I said. It was my job to stay up here and use my water magic, but it wasn't working. And I couldn't just wait and watch.

That was the worst. I had to do something.

My magic was kaput, but I wasn't helpless. I ignored the sick emptiness that seethed in my belly and leapt off the roof, using the windowsills to scramble down the brick front.

Ana followed.

I hit the ground and drew my sword from the ether. The demon woman charged toward me. Her gaze darted from the shop front to me.

I clenched my teeth against the emptiness that filled my chest, and raised my blade.

"Get out of my way," the demon woman snarled. She raised her hands. Yellow magic sparked around them.

"Not a chance in hell. Which is exactly where I'm sending you." I drew my metal shield from the ether and held it up just as she hurled her magic.

It slammed into my shield, throwing me back against the brick wall. Pain flared as the wall crumbled behind me.

I growled and pushed myself off the wall, lunging toward her. Just as she started to hurl another blast of magic, I swiped out with my blade, severing her head from her neck. Blood spurted, splashing my leather jacket.

Gross.

I ignored it and turned, spotting a huge demon with black horns and pale ivory skin. He threw himself against the wooden door of the potion shop, trying to break it down with his shoulder.

"Don't even try it!" I shouted, then ran for him.

Ana sprinted to my side, a dagger clutched in her hand. She hurled it at the demon and nailed him in his bare shoulder. He roared and turned to us, eyes blazing red.

"Hit him again," I said.

She threw her second dagger. It hit him in the chest, right where his heart should be.

But he stayed standing, then charged, his face twisted in a grimace of rage.

"Of *course* his heart is somewhere else," Ana muttered.

"You never can tell with demons." I leapt up as the demon neared, throwing myself toward him.

He reached out, his long claws slicing across my chest. Pain flared, but I ignored it, swiping with my sword.

It sliced across his neck. Blood sprayed, hitting me in the face. I gagged, dropping back onto the ground, then plunged my blade into his gut.

He roared, which was really more of a garbled noise now that I'd destroyed his throat, and tumbled onto his back.

I yanked my sword from his gut as he began to disappear back to the Underworld and turned to Ana.

She wiped blood off her face. "You really need to avoid the arteries."

I pointed to her face. "You missed some."

She scowled and pointed at me. "Ha! As if you should talk."

7

I grinned, though it felt hollow, and turned to survey the scene as my chest ached, the gash seeping blood.

Almost simultaneously, Cade tore the head off a skinny demon with spindly limbs and fangs as long as my hand, while Jude split another one in two. Ali and Haris leapt out of the collapsing bodies of the last two demons.

The street ran red with blood and water, but all of my friends looked okay. Some sported cuts and others limped, but everyone was standing.

Not bad.

Except for the fact that my magic had gone totally kaput.

My shoulders sagged. With heavy feet, I approached my colleagues, who gathered in the street. All around, shopkeepers poked their heads out of doors and windows, surveying the terrain.

Cade came to join me, concern still creasing the brow of his handsome face. I tried to smile, but failed. He stood next to me, tension crackling the air between us. Unusually weak, I leaned against him, absorbing some of his strength.

I might have healing powers now, but it was doing no good in the face of my faltering magic. It was worse than ever.

"Good job, everyone," Cade said. "You did well today."

"I'll take care of the cars," Ammons said. He pointed to Ali and Haris. "You two can help."

The Djinn nodded and joined him.

Jude looked at me. Nerves fluttered in my stomach. Cade might have been in control of the fight operations, but Jude was acting as the trainer today. That meant she was in charge of me, Ana, and the other two trainees.

As far as I could tell, everyone else had done their part.

Only I had failed.

Because I was the DragonGod.

Fancy name for someone who couldn't control their massive freaking magic.

"Well done, you lot." Jude's gaze traveled to me. "But Bree—you were supposed to stay on the roof."

"I wanted to help."

"She did do a good job," Caro said.

Jude sighed. "I know. But with power as strong as yours, you need to be careful. Our roles have reasons, and I know that inaction kills you, but it's for the best when we stick to our assignments. One day, you'll act too quickly and regret it. You wouldn't have gotten that wound if you'd waited."

I didn't mind the wound, but I nodded, knowing she was right. The Protectorate was all about planning and roles—mitigating damage through control. And they had a point.

"We'll meet in my office when we return, Bree," Jude said. "You too, Ana. We have some things to talk about regarding the Rebel Gods."

I nodded. *Good.*

As much as I hated to face the music, I wanted answers. It'd been three days since I'd learned I was a DragonGod and that a group called the Rebel Gods was after me. I'd been trying to get a meeting with Jude or Hedy to learn more, but apparently all I'd had to do was blow my part of a big operation.

The crowd broke up. Ana drifted away to hover by the sidewalk. I shot her a thankful smile, then looked up at Cade.

He was handsome as ever, with his dark hair gleaming in the sun and a black T-shirt stretched over his muscular chest. The two days since our kiss now seemed like an eternity.

Nerves skated across my skin, making me shiver.

"Are you all right?" His gaze traced over my face.

"Probably not."

"Your magic?"

"Yes. Arach told me it would go haywire and start to devour itself, but it's happening sooner than I expected." I reached out for the water in the sewer again, feeling the slightest bit of magic tug in my chest. Dingy water swelled up from the storm drain, then disappeared back underground. "Damn it."

Cade pulled me in for a hug, squeezing me tight. I absorbed his strength, my heart fluttering at the warmth of his muscles.

"You'll figure it out," he said.

"I sure hope Jude has some info for me. I've been waiting two days. No one will talk to me." I pulled back and scowled. They'd made me train as normal, but *nothing* was normal. "And you've been nowhere to be seen."

"You want to pump me for information, too?" A seductive smile tugged at the corner of his lips.

"Maybe." Mostly, I'd just wanted to see him.

But now wasn't the time to talk about that. I wanted answers, and if Jude was about to give them to me, I needed to be there. "I'm going to go. See you later."

He shook his head. "I'm coming with you."

"To the meeting with Jude?"

"Aye. It was delayed because we had to figure out what the hell is going on."

"Well, good. Let's get a move on. Because I want answers about the DragonGods, the Rebel Gods, and how the heck I'm going to keep my magic."

Twenty minutes later, Ana, Cade, and I met Jude and Hedy in the round room. Also known as the war room, it was where they met when things were dire.

Apparently, I qualified. Or at least, my situation did.

The round room was the oldest part of the castle, where the walls were made of heavy stone and the wooden floors were beaten and scratched. Here, tapestries covered the walls, and sconces glowed golden, but it still had a heavy air to it.

Jude and Hedy already sat at the round table. I'd done my best to wipe the demon blood off my face, but I hadn't wanted to waste time changing. Demon blood might be gross, but my thirst for answers outweighed the ick-factor.

Cade, Ana, and I joined them at the table. After our kiss in the pub two days ago, I'd told Cade what I was. He'd been impressed, which—I couldn't lie—I'd totally liked.

"Why did it take so long to have this meeting?" I blurted out. Annoyance—tinged strongly with fear—buzzed in my veins.

"Two days is hardly long." Jude smiled calmly. "You *just* found out you were a DragonGod."

"Two days is long if your magic is devouring itself."

Jude's starry blue eyes darkened with understanding, and perhaps even a bit of sadness. "We weren't expecting your magic to go haywire so quickly."

"It may be because it is so strong," Hedy said. "Each power is fighting for dominance and suppressing the others faster than we expected."

"What do I do?" I asked. If I wanted to stay at the Protectorate, I needed my magic. Not to mention, it felt like hell when it went haywire. Nausea was a constant companion, as was a strong feeling of loss.

"That's what has taken us days to decide," Jude said. "We needed to consult a seer and other resources to determine the right course of action. And to determine if our concerns were warranted."

"And?" Ana asked.

"We'll start with the Rebel Gods," Jude said.

"Yes." I leaned forward, anxious to learn more. The only thing I knew about them was that they had a book with their name on it—in Latin. And a crazy woman with dark magic worked for them, hunting us. "What did you learn?"

"Until now, the Rebel Gods were ancient history, as far as we were concerned. No one has heard from them for hundreds of years. They were an organization that wreaked havoc upon magical populations, stealing and enslaving."

"For what purpose?" I asked. "Did you figure out what was written in the little book that I found a few days ago?"

"Only the cover was in Latin," Hedy said. "The rest was in an unknown language. Florian, the ghost librarian, is working on a translation, but he hasn't found one yet."

"Dang." I frowned. "What did you already know about them?"

"We've never known what their main goal was," Jude said. "Maybe power, or wealth. Their motivations were lost to history. But our seer confirms that they are back—returned to the earth for a specific purpose."

"Hunting us?" I guessed.

Jude inclined her head. "Yes, that could be it. They have shown a marked interest in you. The seer believes that they are a great threat to the Protectorate."

"The curse last week made that pretty clear," I said. Their dark magic had threatened to destroy the whole castle.

"It did." Hedy nodded. "And they were likely after you."

"So I need to go after them," I said. "Bring the fight. I don't like waiting."

Ana huffed a small laugh beside me, one that clearly said, *Ain't that the truth.*

"No, you don't," Jude said. "In some cases, your bravery is a boon. In others, you jump too quickly. It has been your greatest weakness during your training. You always win the fight, Bree. Always. But with magic as strong as yours, you must learn to deploy it only when necessary."

My cheeks heated. But she was right. She'd mentioned this to me before, and I was working on it. But I needed to try harder. I nodded at her.

"Good," Jude said. "If you want to go after the Rebel Gods, you must conquer the magic inside you. The new powers that you are developing are starting to devour each other, leaving you almost helpless. You must learn how to anchor such strong magic."

I shifted uncomfortably, hating that word. I wasn't *helpless*. I had my sword and speed and guts.

But without my magic…

She was right.

I needed my magic. No question.

That made sense. "But *how* do I get control of my magic?"

"Unfortunately, we lack the tools to help," Hedy said. "Yours is an unusual case. We can train you if you have your magic. But if you don't have it, we can do nothing.

"So we suggest that you go to the Cave of Seers," Jude said. "Hopefully, one will appear to you and guide you."

"The Cave of Seers?" I frowned. "What do they do, just hang out there? In a cave?"

Cade chuckled low.

"No." Jude shook her head. "There are no seers on staff here at the Protectorate. Instead, there is a cave at the base of the sea cliffs. Magic imbues the place. A worthy person can enter, and if they are lucky, a seer will appear to them."

"All right." I nodded, liking the sound of this. I'd never met one before, but anyone who could give me advice or directions seemed like a damned good idea.

Hedy consulted her watch, then looked at me. "You still have several hours of daylight left. Long enough to climb down the cliffs. I suggest you get a move on."

～

After a quick shower—during which, the Pugs of Destruction watched me from the sink, the toilet, and the trash bin—I met Cade and Ana at the front of the castle.

A cool, late-summer breeze whipped the blond hair back from Ana's face. Even in August, the highlands were chilly in the evening. In the distance, purple heather stretched across the mountains and the blue sky was dotted with fluffy white clouds.

"Are you ready?" Ana asked.

I zipped up my leather jacket, blocking the breeze. "Definitely. I need answers."

"You'll get them," Cade said. "Come on."

We followed him toward the cliffs, passing by the stone circle that sparked with magic. So far, I'd avoided the circle, a sense of —I don't know, *heaviness*—weighing on me anytime I thought of visiting. There was clearly great magic there—magic that repelled rather than welcomed.

As curious as I might be, I was no dummy. I'd listen to the magic.

The sound of crashing waves grew louder as we neared the edge of the cliffs, and cawing gulls swooped on the air. I hadn't had much chance to come over here, not with training keeping me busy. And evenings were full of visits to the Whisky and Warlock. It was so novel—and so cool—to have a group of friends. So Ana and I had been sticking to them rather than wandering the cliffs like heroines in a gothic romance.

Late afternoon sunlight glittered on the blue sea, which crashed against the cliff a thousand feet below.

Cade stopped near the edge. I inched closer, peering down at a thin strip of beach.

"There's a cave down there," Cade said. "Located in a narrow bay to the left. Climb down the stairs, and you can't miss it."

I eyed the jagged little bits of earth that *sort of* looked like stairs. "Those are the stairs."

"Aye." His brow wrinkled. "Be careful."

I sucked in a ragged breath. "Good thing I'm not afraid of heights."

Just of inaction. And of losing my magic.

So this would be easy-peasy.

"Seriously, be careful," Ana said.

"No need to worry." I gave her a quick hug, then looked at Cade. Now was not the time for a hug. I needed my head clear for this. And we weren't really at that stage yet. Hugging goodbye was relationship stuff.

We were currently at the *staring hotly* phase of this thing.

I saluted, then turned and started down the stairs.

I was only about ten feet down, with the ocean wind buffeting me, when I realized that maybe there was a *little* reason to worry.

These stairs were really more like jutting rocks inching their way down the cliff face. I clung to the stone as I descended, carefully placing each booted foot.

Halfway down, pebbles shifted beneath me. My skin chilled as adrenaline spiked. I scrabbled for a handhold, but I lost my balance.

And fell.

My heart leapt into my throat as I flailed, grasping for the cliff.

All I met was air.

CHAPTER TWO

A scream lodged in my throat as I reached for solid ground. Gravity dragged me down the stairs as the stone cut into my chest and belly.

Finally, I grasped a crevice in the rock, digging my fingertips in. I jerked to a halt, half on and half off the narrow, jagged stairs.

Panting, I clung to the stone, arms shaking and skin chilled with fear. Once my mind had calmed—not much, of course—I scrambled onto the stairs and clung to the stone cliffs. Thank fates, the treads on my boots did a good job of holding onto the rocks.

Why the hell did superhero chicks in movies always wear high heels? What if you had to climb down a mountain cliff to consult some mysterious seers? What then, Hollywood?

I chuckled nervously and shoved the inane thought away. I hadn't been scared of heights before, but that was changing.

Slowly, I got to my feet and continued down the stairs, keeping a wary eye out for bits of gravel.

Gulls swooped by me, eyeing me with beady black eyes as the wind tore my hair from my ponytail. I flattened myself against the cliff and shouted, "I have no bread. Go fishing!"

The gulls flew off, cawing their displeasure to the wind.

"You and me both, guys." Why couldn't the seers hang out in the forest? Or at the Whisky and Warlock?

But then, nothing good ever came easy.

I kept climbing, slowly and steadily, my limbs shaking with the strain. The wind bit at my cheeks, and I focused on it, trying to ignore the danger.

Crashing waves roared as I neared the shore at the bottom. By the time I stumbled onto the stony beach, my heart was pounding and my breath came short.

I took a moment, panting, and enjoyed the sight of the waves. Sparkling blue water rolled against the pebbles, and behind me, the cliffs towered.

"Whew. All right." I dusted off my hands and set off toward the left, seeking the cove that Cade had mentioned.

I found it quickly—hard to miss on a straight beach—and ducked inside. It was short and narrow, a stream of ocean water flowing back, and I followed it along the slender gravel beach.

Soon, I turned a slight corner, and a massive cave loomed in front of me.

"Holy fates." I stopped and stared, awed.

The mouth of the cave was at least three hundred feet tall and just as wide. I could see right in. Cracks in the cave's earthen ceiling allowed light to stream through. Green moss coated the dark stone walls, and the ocean flowed in to form a pool in the middle of the cave. A circle of land surrounded the water.

I hurried into the cave. Magic sparked against my skin, an unfamiliar signature that filled my mind with a calming sense of *knowing*.

Knowing *what* exactly, I had no idea. But since this was the Cave of Seers, it made sense. Seers knew stuff. It was kinda what they did.

It was dark in the cave, with a strange carving on the wall that looked like a large head. Planks of wood were scattered around, old and rotten, along with some metal tools flecked with rust.

How had this place once been used? The tools looked really old.

Slowly, I circled the interior of the cave, searching for a seer or a clue or something.

"Just bits of old stuff," I muttered.

A large rock sat in the middle of the cave, right at the edge of the water, bathed in a pool of sunlight that shined down through a hole in the rock ceiling.

I shrugged and climbed up onto the rock. It looked as promising as anything else.

As soon as I reached the top of the boulder, magic rushed over me, fizzing against my skin like carbonated water. It glowed bright all around me, a golden light that nearly blinded. I fell to my knees, my head spinning.

When my vision cleared, I was no longer in the cave.

A huge tree towered overhead.

No, it wasn't huge. It was ginormous, humongous, ridiculously giant-sized. So big I couldn't see the top, and I couldn't conceive of the circumference. My brain felt like it was short-circuiting as it tried to comprehend.

As far as I could tell, it was as big as the world itself.

Dumbfounded, I searched my surroundings. I no longer sat on the giant rock, but in the middle of a field that butted up to the massive tree.

More than anything, I wanted to fall onto my back and look up at the huge branches that spread overhead, nearly blocking out the sun that filtered through the leaves in shining beams of light.

Joy and a little bit of fear filled my chest.

Then my gaze landed on a small building at the base of the tree. A wooden longhouse, with a turf roof and wooden beams for sides.

I blinked.

Was the house tiny, or normal sized? The tree threw everything out of scale.

Three women walked out of the house, each wearing a dress of green mist that flowed around them. Their golden hair glinted in the streams of sunlight. Then it turned black, then red.

Something tugged me toward them. I followed, struggling to my feet and hurrying forward.

As I neared, I realized that they weren't as young as I'd thought. Nor as old.

In fact, it was nearly impossible to tell their age. Images flashed in their eyes—tiny scenes of life. People and places and animals. Wars and parties and people alone in their houses and so much more. I could stare into them forever.

I sucked in a ragged breath and averted my gaze toward their chins.

Safer that way. I didn't want to spend eternity watching their eyes like they were TVs.

The women were the same size as me, which meant the house wasn't tiny and the tree really was as insanely big as I'd thought. It'd probably take my whole life to walk around it.

I stopped in front of the three women.

The one on the left spoke. "Welcome, Bree Blackwood."

"We are the Norns," said the one in the center.

The Norns. Viking goddesses of fate. Ever since Arach had told me two days ago that I was the Valkyrie DragonGod, magical beneficiary of the Viking god's magic, I'd done some research.

Some of that included the Norns. And the *tree.*

My gaze rose to the tree. "Is this Yggdrasil?"

"It is the world tree, yes."

"And I'm really here?"

The Norn on the right shrugged. "That is up for interpretation. But for now, you are here with us. I am *Urðr.*"

At first, the word was gibberish. But then it sorted itself out in my mind, a strange magic I'd never felt before. Urðr was Old Norse for "that which became or happened."

Apparently I could speak Old Norse now. "You represent the past?"

"Yes." She smiled.

The Norn in the center said, "I am *Verðandi*."

It took a moment, but my mind sorted that one out as well. "You're the present."

"Well done."

"And I am *Skuld*," said the final Norn.

My mind translated. "That which should become, or that needs to occur."

"Precisely. You truly are the Valkyrie." Skuld smiled.

"Yes." Though I *really* didn't feel like it. "I might be inheriting the powers of the Viking gods, but I'm not doing a very good job of holding on to them."

Urðr nodded. "That is normal. I suppose you would like our help determining your fate and how you should go about fixing your power?"

"Yes, *please*. Because I have no idea what to do."

"It won't be easy," Skuld said.

"I'm not afraid of hard work."

"Good." Verðandi nodded. "Now come."

They turned and walked toward the tree, leading me toward a well that I hadn't noticed before. It was small compared to Yggdrasil that I'd never have seen it. Hell, it was a miracle I'd noticed their house. I probably wouldn't have seen an elephant running at me until I'd felt the ground shake.

"Do you always appear to people who come to the Cave of Seers?" I asked.

"We appear to you because you are of the Vikings," Verðandi said.

Fair enough.

We stopped by the well, and Skuld began to turn a crank that lowered a bucket down the shaft. I wasn't sure what they were doing, but I thought I recalled a vague mention of them using a well to help their magic.

Far below the earth, the bucket plopped into the water with a small splash. Then Skuld turned the crank the other way.

Once the bucket was back at the surface, Verðandi pulled it off the hook and placed it on the ground. The three Norns gathered around it and dipped their hands into the water. They murmured to each other, too low for me to hear.

I leaned closer, my heart pounding.

What would they find?

Skuld looked up at me. "You must go to the realm of the Valkyrie and seek your answers."

"The realm of the Valkyrie?" My stomach jumped. "How am I going to get to the land of the gods?"

Verðandi looked at me. "We will provide you with directions. And the tools you need to get there."

"But you must go quickly," Urðr said. "Terrible things happen to those who cannot find an anchor for their magic."

"I know all about that." My magic dying on me today had been miserable. I didn't want any repeats.

"You don't know," Urðr said. "Not really. Show her, Skuld."

Skuld reached for me, her pale, slender hand gleaming with magic.

She touched my arm. Immediately, a sense of emptiness filled me. Death. My soul leaching out of my body. I gasped and doubled over, misery like I'd never known filling every inch of me. I went to my knees, unable to stand.

"This is your future." Skuld's voice resonated with darkness. "If you cannot anchor your magic—*control* your magic—you will lose it forever."

"It feels like my soul is gone." I gasped.

"Exactly." Skuld removed her hand.

I collapsed to my hands and knees. Feeling returned and the

emptiness faded, but the memory was so strong that it made bile rise in my throat.

"You didn't lose your magic before," Urðr said. "You have lost your sonic boom, but your healing power and gift over water are still there. In the battle today, they only faltered, growing weak and useless. When you truly lose your magic—lose *all* of it—you will feel like this. Forever."

"Likely worse," Verðandi said. "When magic goes out of control and your gifts devour each other like snakes in a pit, you will feel worse."

"Worse?" The blood rushed from my head. My life would be over. I'd rather be dead than lose my magic.

Skuld nodded. "So you see why you must go to the realm of the Valkyrie. You will find answers there. The winged warriors will give you the tools to anchor your magic inside you. Then you will be at peace again."

"Though it may take great sacrifice," Urðr said. "It often does."

"Of course." *Good things don't come easy.* "Can you tell me anything about the Rebel Gods?"

I might as well get as much info as I could out of this visit. And anything to distract me from my future would be super great right now.

"You will find answers about them with the Valkyrie. Clues to lead you on your way," Verðandi said. "You are linked with the Rebel Gods, but you must discover how."

"And defeat them," Skuld said. "Your life depends on it. Your sister's life as well."

I nodded. "I will."

"We shall see," Skuld said.

Verðandi punched her lightly on the shoulder. "Have faith, sister."

"She is the Valkyrie DragonGod," Urðr said. "The champion of the Vikings, returned."

Yeah, no pressure.

The three fates stood.

"That is all we can tell you," Skuld said.

Verðandi stooped and dipped her hand into the bucket of water, then pulled out a scroll and a small pouch. She handed both to me. The pouch felt like it had small rocks in it.

"The scroll will guide you to the Valkyrie. The pouch contains helpful tools." She leaned close. "Stick close to your war god. He will be your greatest aid in this. Go only with him."

"Only Cade can come with me?"

"He is the only one who can accompany you where you are going. He is a god. Your sister has not transitioned yet."

"Okay." I nodded. "Thank you."

The Norns nodded, and the tree of life disappeared.

Suddenly, I was back in the cave. It was dark now. I spun in a circle. Moonlight glittered on the water that pooled within the cave. Magic shimmered in the air.

In my hand, I clutched the scroll and the little bag, confirming that this had been no dream.

"Right, then. Off to Valhalla."

∼

I was sweating and exhausted by the time I made it to the top of the cliff. My muscles trembled with strain and my lungs burned. Barely—just barely—I managed to avoid going to my knees.

All those years riding around on the buggy hadn't been the best for my fitness. I could fight. But climb up a cliff like a mountain goat?

Nope.

Cool wind whipped my hair back from my face as I used the moonlight to find my way toward the castle. In fairness, it wasn't hard to miss—giant thing with sparkly golden windows and all.

Warmth enveloped me as soon as I trudged through the massive doors into the entry hall. The scent of mulled wine welcomed from somewhere deep in the kitchens, where Hans occasionally had a kettle brewing regardless of the season.

I ignored it, opening the scroll instead.

Scribbled writing greeted my eyes, something I didn't recognize. I squinted.

Old Norse, maybe?

Had to be. I'd seen it in the books in the library but hadn't learned how to read it yet. I sighed and rerolled the scroll, then dug into the bag of what felt like rocks. I pulled one out.

Yep. A rock.

I turned it over and squinted at the carving on the front. It was a squiggly shape, but hard to tell what exactly. I inspected the rest of the rocks, only able to identify one carving that kinda looked like a face.

"All right, then," I muttered. "Off to the library."

I headed down the hall to Florian's domain. Fortunately, it was evening, so I could expect to find the ghostly night librarian instead of the grumpy Potts, who handled the day shift.

Thank fates for a little luck.

If my luck extended, he'd come out quickly and help me, then I could run all of this by Ana before getting started.

The library contained no people when I entered, but as usual, the fireplaces burst to life, warm orange flame filling the room with a pleasant glow. Two of the Pugs of Destruction slept in beds in front of the largest fireplace on the right wall, but movement on my left caught my eye.

I looked up.

Mayhem fluttered high in the air, a rag in her mouth. She rubbed it against the spines of the books, shaking her little head back and forth.

"Oiling the leather again?" I asked.

She gave a yip, but didn't cease her work.

I grinned. Yesterday, Florian had explained that the spines of the books needed to be oiled to keep the old leather from cracking. It was Mayhem's job to do the books high on the shelves because she had wings.

In return, Florian read bedtime stories out loud to her. Particular favorites were *The Dogs with the Giant Ham* and *Skipping Through Bacon Valley: A Good Dog's Memoir.*

"Florian!" I called, hoping he'd hear me. Sometimes he was off doing who knew what. He certainly never explained why it took him so long to come when I called. The best I ever got was, "Ghosts have lives, too, you know."

Fair enough. Florian had stuff to do.

But I needed help. Pronto.

I found a seat near the fire, wanting to rest my legs for a moment before I headed back into the darker section—the ghost library—to get some books. I might be able to find them on my own without Florian's help, but it was a freaking labyrinth back there.

I'd give him a few moments to show up while I rested my legs. I leaned back in my chair and sighed, enjoying the warmth of the fire.

Ruckus and Chaos snuffled loudly and shifted in their beds, but didn't wake. Chaos's horns glinted in the firelight. I stuffed the carved stones in the pocket of my jeans and unrolled the scroll again, studying it.

After a while, my head began to hurt, but eventually, I swore that the letters began to move.

I blinked. "What the heck?"

Warmth glowed in my chest, almost like magic. But it was a bit different. Subtler. Not the intense *wham!* of developing a new power.

But the letters began to form words I could recognize.

In the cave where one can build and repair, the boat will arise that transports good and fair.

"Holy crap!" I said.

"Can I help you?" Florian's voice sounded.

I jerked my head up. "Florian!"

He looked elegant as always in his eighteenth century apparel. His ruffled cravat was stark white at his neck, and his waistcoat gleamed with blue metallic thread. The wig towering on his head was an unusual choice, since he often went wigless. He must have been out partying with some old-timey friends or something.

He bowed. "Ever at your service, my lady."

I laughed. "You know that's not true."

He sniffed. "Fine, then. Sometimes at your service. When it is convenient."

I grinned.

"But can I help you?" he asked.

"I thought so, but it seems I can read Old Norse now." I recited the first line to him. "Do you know what that means?"

His face brightened. "Norse, you say? But of course I know. That is referring to the Cave of Seers."

"But I was just there."

"Ohhh." He leaned forward. "Did you learn anything good?"

"Maybe, if I can figure out what that line from this scroll means."

He sat in the plush chair across from me and crossed one ankle over his knee, then tapped his elegant fingers on his chin. "Not to worry, my dear. I know what it means. Long before the Cave of Seers was used as a visiting place for seers, the cave was used by Viking seafarers who came to our fair shores. They pulled their boats in for repairs and often overwintered there."

It clicked in my mind. "That's what those tools were. The ones that were scattered around. And the wooden beams."

"Exactly."

"Why didn't you guys ever move them? Surely they should be in a museum."

"Heavens no! Most archaeological sites should be left undisturbed, particularly by laypeople. While it is true that those artifacts are on the surface and subject to the cruel vagaries of weather and fate, we cannot touch them for any reason. Not even for conservation and display. Magic prevents it."

"Oh." I hadn't tried to touch them or pick them up—they weren't mine, after all, and one didn't muck about in magic places getting sticky fingerprints everywhere—but I believed him.

"Yes, well, that is the place where 'one can build and repair,' as the scroll says. And I have to assume that 'the one good and fair' refers to you. You are on a quest, after all. To prove yourself worthy and anchor the magic within you."

"Yep, that's me." I looked down at the scroll. The rest of it seemed quite clear. I snapped it shut and looked up at Florian. "I know what I have to do. Thank you, Florian."

He stood and bowed. "My pleasure to help a DragonGod."

"You helped me before you knew I was a DragonGod."

"Nothing wrong with a little flattery." He grinned cheekily, and the light glinted off his glasses. "I'd help you no matter who you were. But, if you're going to be famous, I'm going to enjoy it."

I grinned. "Night, Florian."

"Goodnight, Bree Blackwood."

I turned and hurried out of the library. I needed to find Ana and tell her what I'd learned. And I needed to find Cade and ask him to come along.

I read the scroll as I walked, picking up more tips from the directions. Apparently the stones would help us along. I patted the bag in my pocket, ensuring they were still there.

I turned the corner toward our apartments and slammed into a broad chest.

Gasping, I stumbled backward. Strong hands caught me before I fell on my butt.

I looked up at the towering figure who radiated warmth and the seductive scent of a storm at sea.

"Cade."

He grinned down at me, handsome as the devil with his dark hair and full lips. "Bree."

"Weren't we in this position just a few days ago?" I asked, embarrassed to hear how breathless I sounded. Visions of our kiss flashed through my mind, warming my skin and sending heat to my cheeks.

"I believe we were." His voice roughened, lowering. Just barely, his hands tightened on my arms. Not enough to hurt, but enough to show he was affected by the memory.

I leaned toward him, my mind buzzing with desire. This was the first moment we'd been alone since our kiss at the Whisky and Warlock. The first moment I'd have a chance to taste him again. Feel him again.

My heart thundered.

Ana appeared in the corner of my vision.

She stopped dead in her tracks, eyes wide. "Oh, sorry!"

I stepped back from Cade, grateful that he was quick to drop his grip.

"Ana. Hey." I smiled, trying to play it cool.

"Hey." Her gaze darted between me and Cade. It was clear she was trying to play it cool, too, but of course there was insatiable curiosity there. If I'd seen her about to smash faces with a sexy god, I'd be pretty interested in getting the scoop myself.

I'd mentioned our brief kiss to her after it had happened— there was no keeping juicy gossip from Ana; she was like a blood-hound—but there'd been no news since then.

"Ana, good to see you," Cade said.

"You, too." She turned to me. "Well, how'd it go in the cave?"

I explained the scroll and the rocks, then turned to Cade. "The Norns said that you could come with me because you're a god and can enter the different realms. Will you?"

"Of course."

"I want to help," Ana said. "I'll come."

"You can't." I frowned at her. "I'm sorry. Since you're not a

DragonGod yet—or haven't come into your powers at least—they said that you wouldn't be able to enter the godly realms."

"Dang." Her shoulders slumped. "I hate you going off to dangerous places alone."

"She won't be alone," Cade said.

"I know, I know." Ana nodded. "It's just that *I* like to be there. We've always had each other's backs. Changing that up is weird. And scary."

I nodded, knowing she'd spend the whole time concerned for me, just like I would if she had to run off to dangerous godly realms without me. I leaned over and hugged her hard.

"Don't worry about me." I pulled away, then smiled at her.

She grinned back at me and nodded, but worry still darkened her eyes.

There was nothing I could do about that, so I let it go and turned to Cade. "Meet tomorrow at sunrise in the entry hall?"

"I'll see you then." He turned and walked away, business as usual.

I, of course, was not businesslike at all. Instead, I mooned after him until he turned the corner.

CHAPTER THREE

The next morning, after swinging by the kitchen to get a cup of coffee and a scone from Hans, the head cook, I hurried to the main hall.

Somehow, I managed not to spill a drip of coffee on my thin black sweater.

Victory!

That didn't save me from the crumbs, but at least they could be brushed off. At one point, a raisin fell into my shirt and I had to stop to shake it out.

A sparkling little mouse scurried out from a hole in the wall and grabbed the dried fruit that dropped to my feet, and then hurried back to the hole in the wall.

"A glitter mouse?" I murmured. "Weird."

The little creature turned back and glared at me with beady black eyes, as if it could understand me.

"Sorry, you're not weird," I said. "You're lovely."

The mouse nodded her little head, which sparkled like diamonds, and carried her raisin off into the hole in the wall.

"All right, then." I popped the last bite of scone into my mouth and kept heading toward the hall.

Cade was waiting for me by the time I arrived. I finished the last sip of my coffee and set the cup on the little tray set into an alcove in the wall. The cup would disappear back to the kitchen, a luxury that delighted me to no end.

"Ready?" Cade asked. He wore the same dark tactical gear as he had last time.

"As I'll ever be."

We walked out into the cobblestone courtyard as the sun peeked over the horizon, lighting the gray morning with a golden glow.

This time, the climb down the cliffside was a little less scary. I still wouldn't do it as a hobby, no matter how nice it would be to stroll the beach down below, but at least I wasn't a shaking mess when I reached the bottom.

"This way." I led him toward the cave, which was still pretty dark this early in the morning.

I stopped near the middle of the cave, gazing around the space, then pulled the bag of carved stones out of my small backpack. I dumped them into my hands, then handed half over to Cade.

"These are supposed to help us," I said.

"How?"

"No idea. But the scroll said it would become obvious."

"All right." He studied his stones.

I bent my head and studied mine. I had four. One looked like an arrow, another like a face, the third like a sun, and the fourth a bird.

I tucked the one with the arrow back into my pocket. If I was understanding the scroll correctly, I'd need that one for later, to help get through the realms of the gods.

The last three were still a mystery though.

I clutched them in my hand and began to pace around the cave. It was a huge space, several hundred feet wide and just as tall. The mouth was enormous, allowing more light to enter as the sun rose.

The carving on the wall that I'd seen yesterday caught my eye. I tilted my head and studied it, then pointed at it. "That looks like one of my carved stones."

Cade joined me, peering up. "We should look for more carvings, then."

"Agreed."

We split up, pacing the space, looking in every nook and cranny for more carvings. On the far left, I found a huge hole in the wall. It led back to an underground spring. The water glittered with bioluminescence, and it allowed me to see that the stream stretched far back into the cave.

Cool.

I turned from it and kept searching. A moment later, I found the sun-shaped inscription high on the wall near the back entrance to the stream.

"I found one!" I called.

"So did I," Cade shouted from across the cave.

Further inspection revealed a tiny little slot in the wall beneath the carving.

I dug the sun stone out of my pocket and put it in the slot. Magic sparked over my fingertips.

"Jackpot." I turned to Cade. "Try to put your stone in a little slot in the rock, if you can find one."

A moment later, he called, "It worked. There's magic here."

It took us fifteen minutes to find the rest of the carvings and insert our little stones into the slots. I didn't find one for the bird stone, but maybe I'd need that for later. As soon as I placed the last one, the air shimmered with magic.

I turned from the cave wall to face the great open space. Magic lit the air, swirling with a golden glow and coalescing on the ground near the tools.

They rose up, dancing on the air, along with the abandoned pieces of wood.

"Amazing," Cade said.

"Just like that movie. *Sleeping Beauty*. Where the fairies make the house clean itself and everything moves around."

In front of us, the wood began to assemble itself on the surface of the water in the middle of the cave. Tools pounded and banged, building the ship in front of our eyes.

First, sparkling magic lifted a heavy piece of wood and connected it to two curved end pieces. Bow and stern, I had to assume. The ship floated in the air as the glittering magic added planks to the sides, each one overlapping another, perfectly fitted and carved. Then some crosswise pieces were added inside. I tilted my head. They looked a bit like slender ribs. Finally, magic added a giant hunk of wood to the middle of the boat. Last, a mast was inserted into it.

Soon, a complete Viking ship had built itself for us.

"Holy fates," I breathed.

Then it drifted on the surface of the water, headed toward the stream that stretched back deeper into the cave.

"Uh-oh. Come on!" I ran after the boat.

Cade caught up to me as I hurried to the edge of the water, where the boat waited. Very convenient.

I leapt inside, stumbling a bit, then righted myself.

Cade, of course, was graceful as ever.

As soon as he was in the boat, it took off, drifting down the glittering water that illuminated the cave around us.

"Bioluminescence shouldn't live here," he said.

"That Viking boat shouldn't have built itself for us." I shrugged. "Magic."

He grinned.

The ether sucked us through. I gasped, reaching out for Cade. My hand met his strong arm, and I clung to him. He gripped me around the waist as the boat rocked through the ether.

A moment later, the sun blazed in our eyes.

Yggdrasil rose tall in front of us, so impossibly huge that I still couldn't conceive of it even though I'd been here yesterday.

"Fates of all," Cade murmured. "The World Tree."

"It's something, isn't it?" I studied our surroundings. I could no longer see the Norns' cottage or their well, which meant that the river had delivered us somewhere else along the base of the great tree.

Fields stretched out around us, and the bottom of the tree was ridged with valleys made by the roots sinking into the earth. We floated on a river that drifted lazily toward Yggdrasil. The boat didn't seem to need any propulsion because it moved along without using the sail or the oars resting against the sides.

"From what I've learned, there are nine realms of the Viking world," I said. "We were on Midgard, where mortals live. Now we have to make it to the realm of the Valkyrie. But to do that, we must pass through several other realms, going higher and higher up the World Tree."

"Do you know where we start?"

I pulled the scroll out of my bag just to confirm, then looked up at him. "We must find Hverglemir, the Roaring Kettle. Also known as the Source of Many Rivers. It will take us to the next realm."

"Does it say which realm that is?" Cade asked.

"Unfortunately not." Which was really very unfortunate. Some of the realms were supposed to be great. Others, not so much.

The river wound around the huge roots that sank into the ground. They rose like mountains on either side of us.

As we rounded a bend, something massive shifted in front of us.

One of the roots was alive!

A huge serpent's head turned toward us. Gleaming green eyes pierced me where I stood, and a tongue flicked out. It looked almost like a dragon, actually.

To the left of the serpent, a huge eagle turned to look at me. Surprise widened the eagle's eyes, and it hopped behind the serpent's coils. Or maybe they were roots? Either way, the bird was definitely hiding.

"I am Níðhöggr. What do you want here?" the serpent hissed.

"Um, I'm Bree Blackwood." I pointed to Cade. "That's Cade." I didn't mention that he was the Celtic God of War. Better not to mention anything violent in front of a serpent who probably considered me a snack. "I've been given a map by the Norns to take me to the realm of the Valkyrie."

Interest gleamed in the serpent's eyes. "The Valkyrie Dragon-God. How interessssting."

"Thanks. Could you tell us where Hverglemir is located?"

He nodded, jerking his head toward the right, in the direction that the water was heading. "Just down that way. Get a move on."

"Thank you." The nervous sweat that beaded on my brow cooled as we drifted by the serpent.

His green eyes sparked with interest as we passed. "Go on, now."

"Yep. We are." I gestured awkwardly at the water. "Just as fast as the water will take us."

"Hmmm." The serpent shifted, a gesture that would almost strike me as nervous.

That was weird. Did he want us gone?

At least he didn't seem inclined to attack or anything. All the same, I stayed tense. Not that I could fight him. His head was the size of a football stadium.

But I'd go down swinging.

I watched him as we drifted out of sight, waving goodbye.

Finally, he was gone.

My shoulders slumped, and adrenaline drained from my muscles, leaving me shaky.

"He was nice," Cade said.

"Yeah." I laughed. "Still scary though."

"Giant serpents usually are." He walked toward the bow of the ship to look out over the twisty river that wound around the trunk of the tree. "Why was he with an eagle? Do serpents and birds usually get along?"

The memory of the eagle hiding himself flashed in my mind, along with a story I'd read. "Yeah, that's really weird, actually. The only eagle that I know of is the one who lives at the top of the tree, while Níðhöggr, the serpent, lives at the bottom."

"But now they're together."

"Seems so."

The sound of roaring waves caught my ear, and I leaned over to try to see around the bend.

A moment later, massive rapids came into view, the water white and roiling. It splashed and bubbled as boulders broke up the tranquility.

"We're nearing the central rapids," I said. More rivers poured into the area. Or out of it?

Whatever the case, our boat was shooting towards it.

"Down!" Cade said.

I threw myself to the deck, huddling near the mast. Cade joined me, wrapping his big body around mine.

Protecting me?

My chest warmed.

The boat bucked and thrashed, throwing us up into the air. We went airborne for a second, then crashed down on the deck. The rollicking ride continued as the boat hurtled through the rapids.

Then everything went dark.

Heat blazed.

The ride smoothed out.

I shook my head, trying to clear my vision, and shoved at Cade. "Move it."

He grunted and lifted himself, rising gracefully. I scrambled to my feet, my heart plummeting as I took in our surroundings.

The air was boiling hot, and the river bubbled. Steam sizzled where the water hit the shore.

"Is that lava?" I pointed to the crumbly, blackened shore.

"I believe so." Cade drew his sword and shield from the ether.

I squinted through the steam that rose up wherever the river hit the molten magma. All around, it was dark. The only light was provided by the lava that glowed red. The land in the distance gleamed crimson and black, like deadly waves.

"How has this water not evaporated?" I asked. It was just a river. A wide one, but there was more lava here than water, and the heat was unbearable.

"Magic," Cade said.

I grinned at his repetition of my word, though it didn't lighten my nerves.

"This has to be Muspell, the land of the Fire Giants," I said.

"It feels safe to assume that."

"I don't know much about them." The scroll hadn't given explicit explanation of what would happen as I went through the realms—just that I had to make it through, continuing on my journey up the World Tree and through the godly realms until I reached that of the Valkyrie, which was near the top. The water had led us though some kind of portal, which had taken us to this realm.

"At least the boat is still moving."

"We're supposed to stay with it until it leaves us, I think."

"Leaves us?"

"I have no idea what that means, actually. I doubt it's good." I drew my sword, not sure that I could actually fight a Fire Giant with a sword. But it was my safety blanket, and I wanted to clutch it tight.

When the roar rent the night, I jumped. The sound vibrated in my chest, like I was hugging a jet engine.

I spun around, searching for the source of the noise.

The monster grew out of the ground a hundred yards ahead

of us, forming from the lava itself—red and black and terrifying. Blazing ruby eyes sought me out, and the beast raised its fist as it howled.

My stomach plunged as it ran forward, pounding toward us. Eighty yards away.

Sixty.

Forty.

Sweat broke out on my brow.

As I tried to call on the water around me, hoping to use it to douse the giant's heat, Cade hurled his silver shield at the giant's head.

The metal gleamed as it flew and sliced through the giant's neck, sending the head flying and the body toppling to the ground. The crash made the land shake and the water around us thrash.

My magic struggled within me, but I managed to get ahold of the water as another giant built itself out of the lava on the ground. Then another.

And another.

"Oh fates." I aimed for the nearest giant, then shouted at Cade, "Take the far ones!"

"On it."

His shield flew through the air as my water rose up in a wave. It was a careful balance not to take all the water from the river and leave us stranded on the bottom. We had to keep traveling, hopefully far away from these beasts.

My wave crashed against the giant, sizzling and steaming.

The massive creature stumbled, almost going to its knees. The molten lava hardened to black stone, making him brittle and unsteady on his feet.

Yes!

Then the creature righted itself, picking up its pace as it hurtled toward me.

Crap! "They're too strong!"

My water wouldn't work against lava. Not unless I had an ocean to draw from. Which I didn't. And from the way my magic struggled inside of me, weak and temperamental, I probably didn't have the control for an ocean anyway.

"And there are too many." Cade caught the shield that had returned to him and pointed toward the others. They raced for us, thundering across the ground as we floated by on the river.

Going too slowly. Like we were vacationing at a hotel with a Lazy River pool.

In hell.

Cade hurled his shield again. As it beheaded another giant, my mind raced.

How could I fight them? Not with a sword—they were a hundred feet tall and made of molten rock. Nor with water.

Cade caught his shield on the return.

And the earth dropped out from under us.

CHAPTER FOUR

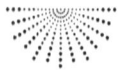

We plummeted into darkness. I screamed, stumbled, then fell to my butt.

I glued myself to the wood as the boat shot through darkness, feeling like it was going down a massive waterslide.

Yes, this was better. Clinging to the hull of the boat was definitely the way to go.

"Cade!"

"I'm here! Are you all right?"

I couldn't see him in the dark, but as long as I was on the boat and could feel the comfort of the hard wooden deck, I could keep my wits about me. "Yeah. Fine! Where are we?"

"No idea."

Slowly, my eyes adjusted as we sped along on an underground river. There was a tiny bit of light—I had no idea from where—that revealed the pocked, glassy black surface of the walls.

"Holy fates, I think we're in a lava tube," I said.

"The dried out tubes from old volcanic activity?" Cade asked.

"The very same." I grinned as I slowly scrambled to a crouch. "Maybe that's the last we've seen of the Fire Giants."

"Somehow, I doubt it."

"Yeah." He had a point. Nothing was easy when you were on a quest. I'd read enough stories in the library lately to understand that.

A moment later, we hurtled out of the tube, back onto the glowing red wasteland. Immediately, giants surged out of the ground around us, rising tall and angry. They roared, sounding like a choral arrangement from hell, and charged.

"Oh, fates!" Desperate, I called on my magic, scrambling for whatever I had.

Maybe I could dredge up a bit of my old sonic boom if the healing and water power hadn't totally crushed it. That would do the trick!

But it stayed dormant inside me. Cold and empty where it had once been.

Cade hurled his shield, beheading two of the giants. Unfortunately, there were three more where they'd come from, running toward us on sturdy legs the size of office buildings.

I reached for my magic, clawing for it as sweat dripped down my temples. It thrashed inside me, then flared to life, an explosion of power inside my chest.

I stumbled, gasping, as the magic tore through me. It filled my body and my mind, an ephemeral thing that made no sense at all.

It felt like a trick.

Like it was there one moment and gone the next. It flitted around inside me.

Cunning, it whispered. *Trickery.*

"What?" I demanded, gasping.

Trick them. Fool them. Create the world as you would like. The voice hissed in my mind, power and strength and cunning and guile. *Trick them.*

"What does that mean?" I cried.

Magic glittered at my fingertips. In my mind, it was as if I could see it sparkling through my brain, weaving between synapses and firing up neural pathways.

I had to do this with my mind, I realized.

Cunning and guile and trickery.

Loki!

This was Loki's power.

Holy fates, that was a big one.

How to trick a Fire Giant?

Beside me, Cade hurled his shield, time and again. But there were more and more giants, coming too fast for him to defeat.

What did they want more than us?

My mind raced, trying to remember what I'd read about Viking lore in the library. Thank fates for Florian and his books. And my long-banked desire to learn.

The Fire Giants hated the Ice Giants above all else.

That was it!

I imagined the Ice Giants as I'd seen them once before, when I'd fought with my friend Nix. Towering and angular, made of icicles and slabs of frozen water. I envisioned them appearing to the left, away from Cade and me. A whole group of them.

They appeared out of nowhere, towering as high as the Fire Giants and gleaming an icy blue in the red light of the lava.

And they didn't melt.

Please don't notice that, Fire Giants.

"Where did they come from?" Cade shouted.

I ignored him, unable to speak and also focus enough energy on keeping the ice giants visible. They shimmered occasionally, every time I lost a bit of control of my power.

But when the first Fire Giant noticed the Ice Giants, his roar ripped through the air like a victory song.

The Fire Giant spun on his heel and pounded away from us, racing for his greatest enemy. The others followed, their footsteps shaking the ground.

Oh crap!

The Ice Giants needed to run away. Else the Fire Giants

would realize they were fake. I imagine the Ice Giants jumping with surprise, then turning and fleeing from the Fire Giants.

The result was a little weird looking—like a cartoon mouse spotting a cat—but the apparent fright seemed to excite the Fire Giants, who only roared louder.

"You're doing this," Cade said.

"Yep." I gritted the word out through clenched teeth, keeping the magic going.

When the boat dropped into another lava tube, I lost hold of the magic. My heart jumped as we fell, but at least this time I knew what it was.

I dropped low and clung to the deck.

"Are you all right?" Cade asked.

"Yeah."

But the boat started going faster and faster. By the time the river plowed back onto the glowing red plain, my stomach was turning.

The Fire Giants were still searching for the Ice Giants, who had disappeared, when my magic had faltered. Before I could light it up again, the boat accelerated.

"Brace yourself!" Cade shouted.

I turned, looking toward the bow. A shimmery dark stain on the air blocked the river.

A wall. A portal?

I had no idea. But I threw myself back to the deck alongside Cade.

Then the boat slammed into the wall, splintering into a thousand pieces and throwing us into the air.

I tumbled for what felt like days, hours. A half second. It was impossible to say.

Then I crashed to the ground. Pain flared. Cade sprawled next to me. Aching, I climbed to my feet.

It was brighter here, wherever this was.

Cade rose. "That was a portal."

"Or a strange exit." I spun in a circle.

We stood on rough ground that looked like giant bark. The light was bright, though I could see no sun, and giant leaves fluttered overhead in the breeze.

"We're on one of Yggdrasil's higher branches," I said.

"Do you know which world we go to next?" he asked.

"No." I pulled the scroll out of the bag on my back. It was now crumpled and bent, but still legible. I'd just started to read—and spotted the word *Huginn*—when a strange sound filled the air. Like the flapping of massive wings.

I looked up.

A huge raven landed on the branch next to us. It was easily three times as tall as Cade, with gleaming black feathers and shiny jet eyes. It cawed and dipped its head.

"Hello, Huginn," I said. "You're Odin's raven, aren't you?"

The bird cawed again.

"I think he's here to give us a ride," I said to Cade.

"You have the assistance of the Old Father?"

I nodded, recalling that Old Father was one of Odin's nicknames.

Huginn cawed again, pointing his beak at me.

I glanced down at the scroll and caught the word for payment. And stone. I dug into my pocket for the remaining two stones, found the one with the bird on it, then handed it over. "For you."

Huginn bowed his head and stuck out his giant clawed foot. I dropped the stone in, and his toes curled around it. Then he bent low enough for us to climb on.

"This is wild." I grinned at Cade, then scrambled up onto the giant raven. It was a bit weird to sit on feathers, but cool.

Cade climbed up behind me.

I gripped the feathers and crouched low. "We're ready!"

Huginn took off into the air, great wings carrying us high. The wind whipped my hair back from my face, and I laughed, joy filling me. I looked behind me at Cade and grinned. He looked happy, too.

Huginn carried us high up into the giant ash tree, gracefully dodging leaves and smaller branches, which were the size of great highways in huge cities.

Finally, Huginn landed on another branch, hopping to a stop. Once we were stable, I climbed off, hair windblown and cheeks cool from the breeze. Cade followed.

"Thank you, Huginn."

The bird cawed and took off. I turned in a circle, trying to figure out where to go next. The branch was so wide that I couldn't see over either end. It had to be miles across. In the distance, the tree trunk rose high into the air.

"Which way?" Cade asked.

I consulted the scroll once again, remembering something I'd read about a compass stone. Was this where I should use it?

I skimmed the text. Yep. Compass stone.

I pulled the last rock out of my pocket and held it flat in my palm. The carved arrow spun on the stone, which should be impossible since it wasn't a separate piece of the rock—it was actually carved into the rock itself.

But I was also standing on Yggdrasil, the world tree of the Norse gods, so things were already beyond belief. This stone wasn't nearly the weirdest thing that would happen here.

The arrow stopped spinning, facing toward the trunk. I pointed. "That way."

We set off across the tree limb, making our way over uneven ground made of giant bark. The bark was so jagged that it was almost like walking across broken land struck through with crevasses and ditches. I had to hop over those as often as I walked with regular steps.

"This is truly amazing," Cade said.

"Don't you go to the world of the Celtic gods?" I asked.

"No, never. Earthwalking gods are reincarnates. My job is

here, on earth. Though I probably could access the Celtic godly realm, I'm not sure how."

"Do you wish you could visit?"

"Aye. I'd like to meet more people like myself." He looked at me. "But then, you and Ana are similar in power."

I grinned. "That doesn't make us like brother and sister, right? I don't want this thing between us to go the way of Luke and Leia."

He grimaced slightly. "No. Not you, at least. Ana, perhaps. There is a sibling-like feeling for her. But not you. You're a Viking."

"I am, aren't I?" It was really freaking cool, now that I thought of it. And Ana would be a DragonGod from another mythos. "A Valkyrie. A DragonGod."

"Exactly. With the potential to be one of the most powerful supernaturals in the world. Have you gained the power of illusion? Because those Ice Giants didn't melt when they arrived in Muspell. And the timing was just too convenient."

I nodded. "Yes. I think it's a power from Loki, the trickster god."

His brows rose. "Loki?"

"Yeah, crazy, right?"

"Illusion is powerful."

"I know. But my water power is faltering. And my healing will go soon, too. It seems that with every new power that the gods gift to me, another one gets squashed or driven away. I can't count on this one sticking around."

"But you can count on fixing your magic. You can do that, Bree."

"Thanks." My heart warmed, but we'd reached the massive trunk of the tree. No more time to talk. I looked down at the arrow. "It's still pointing to the trunk."

"There may be an entrance." He went left, towards a shadowed area on the trunk, which was so big that it didn't even look like it curved around. It was just a wall made of massive bark, with nooks and crannies. "Here."

I joined him. There, in the shadows of one of the nooks, the air shimmered darkly. Like the same portal that had led us out of Muspell.

I tucked the compass stone safely in my pocket and stowed the scroll in my backpack. "Let's go."

We stepped up to the shimmery dark air that led into the nook between the bark. It was big enough for us to walk in side by side, so I reached for Cade's hand.

He gripped mine, and counted down.

On one, we stepped through.

Into hell.

The world we entered was dark—almost like it was underground. Or in a giant cave. High above, the air glowed golden, as if the sky were on fire. Though there was no red lava on the ground, the earth was black and jagged. It was like a bomb had exploded on a field of granite, tossing the rocks up into the air and letting them fall down as piles of debris.

There were no paths or roads that I could see, just jagged earth that we'd have to weave our way around.

"I have a feeling that this place will be no more welcoming than Muspell," Cade said.

"Probably worse." I looked back up at the orange sky. It cast a warm glow on the ground below, but not in a welcoming way. "The sky looks like a fake tan that's on fire."

Cade chuckled.

I dug into my pocket for the compass stone. It spun, then pointed forward. "Let's go. Hopefully we can make it through this world without being caught."

"Do you have any idea where we might be?"

"It's scary enough to be hell, but I think that's supposed to be under the tree. So maybe it's Svartálfar, land of the Dökkálfar, the Dark Elves."

He frowned. "Not good."

"No, they're scary bastards, from what I've read." I set off across the uneven ground, weaving my way between the jagged stones that pierced the sky. They rose tall on either side of me, some only six feet tall and others twenty.

We walked in silence, all our effort focused on finding the easiest path through this miserable hellscape.

I strained to hear every little thing, feel every little prick of magic in the air. There was no way this would be as easy as walking. The tension made my heart race and nerves jump.

I hated the waiting. I wanted to jump, fight, go for it.

Something was going to come for us—but what?

When the loud growl sounded, the weirdest sense of relief and terror shot through me. It felt like a relaxing of my muscles combined with a sick surge of adrenaline through my veins.

"Cade," I whispered.

"I hear it."

We stopped dead, then pressed our backs against a wall of rock and scanned our surroundings.

The dim orange light cast hundreds of shadows at the bases of the jagged rocks, making it difficult to see what was coming.

But by the time the monster appeared, I was shocked that I'd missed it. The wolf was way too big to slink about in the shadows of the rocks. It was easily six times the size of a normal wolf, with jet black fur and gleaming yellow eyes.

Magic sparked around it, silver bursts of light.

"It must be Sköll or Hati, the sons of Fenrir, the great wolf," I said.

Cade nodded. "At least I stand a chance against this one. Fenrir would do me in."

"Fenrir is the size of a castle."

Cade's magic shimmered around him, and a moment later, he transformed into a giant gray wolf. He was still smaller than the other wolf, but that didn't stop him from growling low in his throat and charging the bigger beast.

My heart thundered as he ran, powerful legs carrying him around the jagged rocks.

Sköll, which seemed like the right name for him, bared his fangs and crouched low, the fur rising at his hackles. Cade rushed him, huge feet eating up the earth as he ran.

Sköll leapt for Cade, and the two collided in a clash of fur and fangs. The growling was loud enough to vibrate through my chest, and the fight was fierce. They tore at each other, grappling on the ground.

Fear raced through my veins like acid. I drew my sword and shield from the ether. There was no way I could let Cade take on this giant wolf alone.

He was holding his own, tearing at Sköll's shoulder with his white fangs, but Sköll leaned over and got one of Cade's fore-limbs between his teeth.

He chomped down. I winced, feeling the pain as if it were my own.

My mind buzzed and my skin chilled as a desperate desire to *do* something streaked through me. But what?

I couldn't throw myself between them. I'd be wolf chow.

Sköll used his great weight to roll Cade beneath him. They were almost evenly matched, but I couldn't rely on that.

A jagged outcropping of rock towered over the two figures. I eyed it briefly, long enough to determine that my plan was only slightly insane but definitely better than throwing myself between two giant wolves, and raced for it.

I scrambled up the side of the jagged rock, struggling to main-tain my balance while gripping my sword and shield instead of the ground beneath me. The wolves thrashed on the ground below, growling and tearing at each other.

I ran to the edge of the stone and jumped, sailing through the air. *This was nuts!*

CHAPTER FIVE

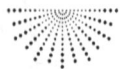

I landed on the back of Sköll, my blade pointed downward. It sliced through his shoulder, driving deep.

The wolf howled and reared. I barely managed to cling to his massive back with my knees as I yanked the sword from his shoulder and stabbed again. His roar rent the night. He surged up on his back feet, releasing Cade from beneath him and throwing me off his back.

My sword pulled free of his muscles, and I tumbled off him, landing with a hard crash on the ground.

Next to me, Cade leapt up, growling and snapping his teeth as he lunged for Sköll. I stumbled to my feet and raised my sword, trying to look as big and threatening as possible.

Ha. As if that would fool Sköll.

The great wolf growled once at Cade, rage in his eyes, then turned and ran off into the night.

My muscles sagged, and I dropped my arms to my side. "Holy crap."

Panting, I bent over, catching my breath. Fear bubbled through me, and I laughed, sounding crazy to my own ears.

Magic shimmered around Cade, and he shifted back to

human. I stood, catching sight of his bleeding and mangled arm. More blood oozed from his side and the gash on his thigh.

Worry tugged at my chest. "He got you good."

Cade winced, raising his arm to inspect it. "His jaws were fierce. You shouldn't have fought the wolf."

"Ha. As if I'd leave you." I inspected his wound. Bile rose in my throat at the flash of white between the destroyed flesh of his arm. Broken.

"Let me help." I stashed my sword and shield in the ether and raised my hand to hover over his arm.

"No, it's unnecessary."

"*You* need it. I can see your *bones*."

He chuckled, then winced. "I can heal myself, remember?"

"Oh, right. Of course." It had just been the weird poison in the Fae realm he hadn't been able to heal from. But I was so ready to jump in and save him that I'd forgotten.

Yeah, I was definitely smitten with Cade.

I waited as his magic surged. The lines on his face relaxed as the pain faded, and his muscles unbunched. The torn skin and broken bone knit back together in front of my eyes.

"Wow, you're good at that," I said.

"Practice."

"Yeah, I guess you've been doing this a while, huh?" I recalled his side gig fighting in wars for the good guys. He must have been injured a lot.

He just shrugged.

Now was not the time to poke around for more information, so I dug the compass stone from my pocket. It pointed us in the right direction, and we set off. I kept it gripped in one hand, with my sword gripped in the other. Best to be prepared.

The landscape didn't change much as we walked, but eventually, the stone beneath our feet turned to dirt. There were still jagged rocks all around, but there were fewer.

In the distance, light glowed a bit more brightly. I pointed. "What do you think that is?"

Cade frowned. "Hate to say it, but probably a settlement."

"Settlement of *what*, I don't want to know."

"Agreed. If we can just—"

He stopped talking as the ground shifted beneath us. Magic sparked on my skin, a warning that made my heart jump into my throat.

Then a root burst out of the earth. There were no trees for miles, from what I could see, but it definitely looked like a root.

Until it twisted into the shape of some kind of monster, with claws and fangs made of rock. It swiped out an arm, rock-claws glinting.

Cade swung his sword, severing the arm. He lunged, taking the head next.

I shoved the compass stone into my pocket and raised my sword. The next monster surged out of the dirt.

It lunged for me, and I beheaded it with a swipe of my blade. The featureless head tumbled to the ground, and the body followed. We fought our way through a field of the creatures, slicing and swiping as we ran.

Their claws dug into my flesh as they burst from the ground, somehow knowing just where I would run. They could probably feel me through the dirt. Every inch of me burned with pain as blood slicked my skin and dampened my clothes.

My sword glinted in the weird orange light from the fiery sky above as I beheaded monster after monster.

At my side, Cade was just as productive, leaving a trail of inhuman bodies. They didn't bleed or make any noise.

My lungs were burning by the time the monsters finally stopped leaping out of the ground. We were nearly to a lake that gleamed black and slick. I stopped, panting.

Cade halted next to me, his wary gaze scanning the terrain that we'd left behind. The bodies of the monsters looked like broken sticks now. Totally unrecognizable as the beasts that had clawed at my flesh.

If the cuts all over my body didn't hurt like hell, I might have thought I'd imagined the monsters. Cade didn't look much better, his neck and hands slicked red with blood.

Why the hell had the monsters stopped?

The sudden thought made dread rise in my chest. Slowly, I turned to face the lake. Was there something here that scared *them*?

A head broke the surface of the water, black hair smooth against the skull. Huge dark eyes peered up from the water, stark against pale white skin.

The creature's head was only half out of the water, hair floating around it like weeds. Its eyes were glued to me.

I swallowed hard, my skin gone cold. It looked like the creepy girl from that horror movie where she climbs out of the TV, except this creature was submerged in inky water, staring at me with evil gleaming in its dark eyes.

"Stay away from the water," I said. "That's the Nökken. It will try to drown you."

"You don't need to tell me twice," he said.

As quickly as we could, we made our way around the dark lake. The Nökken followed us with its eyes, spinning in the water to keep sight of us. My heart thundered louder with every step. The Nökken's steady silence and stillness were creepier than an outright attack.

Tension had tightened every muscle in my body by the time I made it to the far side of the lake.

On this side, we were closer to the glowing light that hovered on the far horizon—the settlement.

The Nökken still watched us.

I was about to dig into my pocket for the compass stone when shouts sounded.

I jumped. Cade's gaze collided with mine.

"Hide," he mouthed.

I nodded, and we hurried to a tumbled pile of rocks and pressed ourselves into a crevice.

The shouts had gone silent, but I swore I'd heard at least three different voices. Who could they be?

I glanced at Cade, who was so close I could smell his storm-at-sea scent overlaid with the tang of his blood. It turned my stomach.

We could fight them. Or should we just hide?

Something heavy slammed over me.

A net!

I thrashed, trying to break free, but magic imbued the net, binding me tight. Next to me, Cade couldn't even move. *I* couldn't move.

I'd only been thrashing inside my mind.

A silent scream tore through my head, a dull roar brought on by the sheer horror of being incapacitated.

This was worse than *anything*.

When the figures appeared in front of us, I shuddered internally, still bound by the net.

They were tall and slender, with the pointed ears of the elves. Their hair was black as pitch, along with their eyes. Their skin was an eerie ice white, shot through with black veins. Strange clothes of textured black leather helped them blend into the dark surroundings.

Six of them inspected us, their gazes traveling over our bloody forms. Their noses wrinkled.

Without speaking, one of them flicked a finger, and we rose into the air, carried by the net.

My heart thundered like a bomb in my head as I tried to fight my way free. But I didn't move an inch.

We floated along behind the silent contingent of Dark Elves. The Dökkálfar, they were called. Dangerous. Deadly. That meant I was right—this was the realm Svartálfar.

If only we'd gone to the realm of the Light Elves.

But nope!

Dark Elves for us.

My mind raced as we floated along, heading toward the glow on the horizon. We shifted in the air slightly so that I could see back the way we'd come. Behind us, a small ghostly white light flickered around the jagged rocks.

Following us?

I squinted toward it, but it disappeared.

Damn.

We shifted again as the elves moved our party around a large collection of rocks. With my neck frozen stiff, I could only see in the direction that they pointed us.

This time when I looked forward, the glow on the horizon had been replaced by a massive black castle. It was as ornate as a wedding cake for a princess, but entirely black, with dozens of turrets and bridges and twisty bits and flags. Light glowed from it, orange and bright.

Like flame.

Fear iced my skin.

I did *not* want to go in there.

Holy fates, I did not.

But they dragged us ever closer, and bile rose in my throat. The moat surrounding the castle bubbled like black oil, and the massive gate creaked as it opened. How would one ever escape?

We wouldn't.

The courtyard was full of Dark Elves, all of them turning to watch us with their dead black eyes. Their skin was so pale that they looked like snow. One of them hissed at us, revealing long fangs.

Oh crap oh crap oh crap.

Frozen like this, unable to fight... It was a nightmare.

We floated through an ornate entry hall that was done entirely in shining black onyx, then into a long room with an arched ceiling. The floor was threaded with veins of gold. It reminded me of a fancy cathedral back on Earth, but when we were dumped onto the floor in front of a throne built of bones, all memory of church faded from my mind.

The elf that stared down at us was bigger than the rest, his cheeks gaunt and his eyes burning bright. He was draped in gold, gleaming like the sun.

"What do we have here?" His voice hissed like a snake's, sibilant and smooth.

"We found them by the Nökken's pond, my liege," said one of the elves.

At first, I didn't realize that he was speaking Norse. But the confusion in Cade's eyes clued me in.

Apparently I could understand it as well as read it.

The leader pursed his lips as he studied us. "The female feels familiar. Strange."

Those were contradictory terms, but I had no way to correct him when I couldn't move my mouth. Not that it would be a smart thing to do.

The elf king tapped his chin with long fingers as he thought. "Lock them up while I try to determine what to do with trespassers on our land. I will call for the interrogator. He will get answers from them."

The interrogator.

Oh, that sounded *bad.*

"We shall see what he says," the elf king continued. "Perhaps they will go into the mines. Until then, put them in the dungeon."

Something told me the dungeon or the mines were better options than the Dark Elf king figuring out that I was a Valkyrie DragonGod.

We were hoisted into the air by magic and carried from the room. As we drifted away, I stared back at the elf king. His gaze followed me, burning bright.

He'd figure out what I was.

No way I could let that happen.

The six elves accompanied us down to the dungeons. As we floated, the halls shifted. I could feel them moving, swinging through space and tilting up and down. It'd be impossible to find our way out of here.

I swallowed hard as we were taken deeper and deeper into the castle. Strangely enough, the floor down here gleamed with even thicker veins of gold, as if it were coming from the earth itself instead of being laid into the floor during construction. But that was impossible, right?

Except, we weren't even on Earth anymore. Midgard was far way. This was Svartálfar, and anything was possible here.

We reached a heavy iron door, which the lead guard opened with a big iron key. They tossed us in, dragged the net off of us, then slammed the door.

I lay still on the hard ground, gasping. Trying to calm my mind.

Next to me, Cade sat up. He shuddered. "There's something wrong with the air here."

Shaking, I joined him, barely able to keep myself upright.

The room was small, the walls covered in a dark mist. It seeped toward me, chilling my muscles and creeping into my mind.

"Magic," I said.

Cade shuddered again, his face pale. He climbed to his feet and inspected the walls, pressing his hands to the stone. The black mist darkened his skin. He pulled them back.

He went to the door. Tried the handle. Of course it didn't work, but I couldn't blame him for trying.

Then he threw himself against the door, leading with his shoulder. It didn't budge. Again and again, he hurled himself at the iron barrier. The blows were so hard that the entire room shook—but the door didn't break.

"Knock it off!" a voice shouted in Old Norse.

Cade stopped, panting. "What did he say?"

"Knock it off," I translated. "Somehow I can speak Old Norse. The king is calling someone called the interrogator. They'll try to determine why we're here, and then possibly put us in the mines."

"We can't escape from there." Cade was still pale, an unusual sight for the brave god.

I didn't like being locked up, but he was taking this harder. The guy who threw himself at a giant wolf and would fight anything single-handedly did *not* like being locked up. He'd made the damn walls shake with the force of his blows.

I didn't rise—my muscles felt too weak—but I lifted my arms. "Come here."

"Why?"

"We need to figure out how to get out of here, but first, I could use a hug." I didn't say that he could also probably use a hug.

His face softened. He came to sit next to me, and pulled me into his arms. My muscles relaxed. My mind cleared slightly.

"This black mist affects us," I said.

"No kidding. I don't like dungeons." He didn't shudder, but I could hear one in his voice. "But this is worse than most."

"You've spent a lot of time in dungeons?"

"As a child. But that's a story for another time."

My heart ached. I was desperate to ask more, but he was right. We didn't have time for a chat. We had to plan. But I didn't let go of him. Touching him anchored my mind in the real world, farther from the horror of this place and the magic that sought to incapacitate us.

"The mist is a good idea," I said. "It's probably supposed to make us weak and frightened. Ideal prisoners who won't try to escape."

"It won't work. We'll find a way." He was more hopeful now that we were touching. The mist couldn't affect us as strongly like this. He studied the door, brow creased. "It's enchanted, so I can't break it. We need the key."

"Maybe we can ambush the guard."

"We'll have to avoid that net."

"Won't be easy. But maybe—"

A glowing white light drifted through the door. It took me a moment to realize what it was. When I did, my heart leapt, joy flooding through me.

"Mayhem!" I whispered.

The ghostly pug fluttered in front of me, her wings keeping her aloft. Instead of a ham in her mouth, she had a key. *Holy fates!*

"I can't believe this." Stunned, I held out my hand.

She dropped the key into my palm. I still had no idea how a ghost could manipulate objects, but if she could chomp down on a real ham, she could chomp down on a key.

"She stole it from a guard." Cade grinned, giving me an appraising glance. "Mayhem has chosen you."

"What does that mean?"

"I've heard that the Pugs of Destruction occasionally choose a companion. She'll help you from now on."

Mayhem nodded her little head, looking like she wanted to bark but knowing better.

"Thanks, Mayhem. You can eat ham in bed anytime you want."

A doggy smile creased her wrinkled face, and her tongue lolled out of her mouth.

"Let's get out of here," I said.

I broke contact with Cade—immediately feeling more weak and miserable as a result of the magical mist— and stepped up to the door. Mayhem pressed her ghostly form against my hip, her wings fluttering through me.

Cade drew his sword and shield from the ether. I cranked the key in the lock.

It clicked then swung open.

I peeked out into the hall. A form was slumped against the wall on the right. A Dark Elf.

I looked at Mayhem and whispered, "Your work?"

She nodded.

"Do you know how to get out of here?"

She shook her head, her eyes saying, "No freaking clue."

"That's okay." Hopefully the compass stone would help us.

We slipped out into the hall, and I pulled the stone from my pocket. I didn't know how it worked, but I silently begged it to lead us out of here. The needle swung, then pointed us down the hall, away from the passed-out elf.

I drew my sword from the ether, and we hurried along on silent feet. As we ran, the halls changed, shifting and moving.

When a passageway spilled us out into a massive room full of Dark Elves, my heart stopped. They turned to look at us, onyx gazes bright. Over their heads, sharp pikes stuck out of the wall like horrible, deadly decorations.

"Oh, shit." I spun to run back down the hall, but it had disappeared.

There was just wall behind us.

"Double shit." I shoved the stone into my pocket and drew my shield as I turned to face the elves.

Cade hurled his shield, beheading two elves. Their blood sprayed into the air.

One of the elves turned into black mist and hurtled toward me, a ghostly apparition that moved faster than my eyes could follow.

It slammed into me, entering my body with a sickening squelch. My stomach turned and my mind fogged.

Panic raced through my veins.

The shadowy elf was inside of me!

Pain burst through every nerve ending in my body. I raised

my sword, my head turning to find Cade. I stepped toward him, my muscles screaming.

No.

I was going to kill Cade. This elf was going to force me to kill Cade!

CHAPTER SIX

I screamed inside my head, fighting the elf's will. Sickness rose as my muscles twisted.

Mayhem hurtled toward me, her little ghostly form flying as fast as she could. She plunged into my chest, bringing with her the feeling of lightness and joy.

I gasped, suddenly in control again.

The joy disappeared, and I felt Mayhem fly out of my back. It was the weirdest feeling in the world.

She'd driven the elf out.

I spun, catching sight of the elf behind me, in corporeal form, looking shocked. I swung my blade, beheading him. Blood spurted, and I dodged, getting splashed on the cheek.

Panting, I turned to search the room.

"Don't let them fly into you!" I shouted to Cade.

He was fighting two of them. Each threw blasts of black smoke. It seemed that not all of the elves could possess people.

Thank fates.

I lunged for an elf near me, raising my shield to block the shadowy black bomb that he hurled at me. It ricocheted off the shield, but his next shot hit me in the leg.

Pain flared as needles shot into my skin.

I ignored it, leaping toward him. I stumbled on my injured leg, slicing with my sword and delivering a deep gouge to his chest. He hissed, his fangs as pale as his skin, and raised his hand to throw another blast at me.

Desperation gave me speed, and I chopped off his hand, my stomach turning at the sight. He shrieked and stumbled back, and I delivered a killing blow, right to the heart.

I yanked my blade free and turned to the room. Cade fought two elves, while Mayhem flew in circles around the space, pursued by a shadowy black figure that was about her size.

I squinted.

It looked like a dragon made of smoke!

The dragon put on a burst of speed and flew into Mayhem, just like the elf had flown into me. Mayhem stopped flying. She thrashed briefly in the air, then a burst of light flashed around her.

She shot a blast of fire out of her mouth, looked surprised and delighted, then shot another one. She yipped with joy, then flew around the room as fast as she could, aiming straight for the elves who fought Cade.

She blasted fire at one of the elves, who screamed. His hair lit up, and he smacked his head, trying to put out the flame. Mayhem went after the other elf, a look of pure joy on her fire-breathing face.

Holy fates, Mayhem had absorbed the powers of that dragon. She was half dragon now, or something like it. She even kinda looked like a dragon when she shot her flame, her form flickering and changing briefly.

Wow.

Cade loped toward me, deadly grace in the face of battle.

"More will come," he said.

Mayhem fluttered over to us, looking delighted with herself.

"We need to run for it, but we can't have them pursuing us." I searched the room. The bodies scattered around weren't ideal. But maybe if they thought we were dead, too....

My gaze landed on the pikes that stuck out of the wall. They were pretty high up. Someone would need a ladder to reach them, unless they'd been tossed up there.

Oh yeah. That gave me an idea.

"This is going to be weird." I called on my illusion magic, letting it flow through me. I envisioned our bodies impaled on the pikes as if they'd been thrown up there, our blood dripping to the floor.

They appeared, just as I'd envisioned them.

I winced at the sight of myself. But the sight of Cade, broken and bleeding, tore my heart out of my chest. I shuddered and turned to him.

"I can hold that for a while. Long enough to get a head start."

"Good."

Footsteps sounded, running down the hall toward us.

"We need speed now, not stealth." Magic swirled around Cade. He shifted into his wolf form and bent low.

I stashed my sword and shield in the ether and leapt onto his back, clinging to his fur. He raced out of the room, down a wide hall, and away from the oncoming footfalls.

I focused my magic on maintaining the illusion of our dead bodies hanging from the pikes. Hopefully they wouldn't realize we weren't there until they climbed up and tried to retrieve us.

I had no idea if it was working since I wasn't there to see it, but I hoped with everything I had in me.

Mayhem flew at our side as I dug into my pocket for the compass stone. I pulled it out, and started giving Cade directions. His speed made up for any loss of stealth, and we made good time through the moving hallways of the creepy castle.

When we spilled out into a back courtyard, I was grateful to see that it was empty. A back gate was all that stood between us and freedom.

But it was as massive and sturdy as the front gate.

Damn it.

"How will we get out?" I muttered.

Mayhem shot forward, flying through the air. She flickered into her dragon form, an illusion that was really weird. Fire burst from her mouth, and she melted the gate.

Cade leapt through, his giant wolf form barely making it.

I wanted to whoop with victory, but restrained myself.

We raced across the jagged earth, following the compass stone as we ran. Wind tore at my hair as Cade sprinted along, his great strides eating up the ground. Mayhem flew alongside, zipping around rocks and shooting fire.

I turned around, searching the castle that grew smaller in the distance.

Hopefully my trick had worked. By the time they realized our bodies weren't real, we'd be out of this realm. As long as we didn't run straight into any dangers.

That was the risk with going as fast as we were, but we had to take it.

I clung to Cade, crouched low over his warm body as his muscles moved beneath me. Every part of me ached from my wounds. Honestly, I probably wouldn't have been able to walk if he didn't carry me. They were slowly healing from my innate power, but it was taking time. I wasn't willing to waste what I had in case I needed it later.

Finally, we neared a gleaming black portal. The compass stone pointed right for it.

"The exit!" I shouted.

Cade leapt through it, Mayhem at our side.

We tumbled through space and rolled to a stop on one of the branches of Yggdrasil. Panting, I lay on my back, staring up at the sky and massive leaves.

Next to me, Cade shifted back into his human form, his magic gleaming around him.

"Nicely done," he said.

"You got us out of there."

"I'd give Mayhem the credit for that."

The ghostly PugDragon zipped around the air, blowing fire as she did loop-de-loops.

"I think she absorbed some kind of shadowy elf dragon thing. Or its powers, at least."

"That wouldn't surprise me. The Pugs of Destruction have powerful magic."

"Well, it helped."

"And what do you think you are doing in my tree?" The voice came from behind, a strange, high-pitched sound.

I sat up and turned, not surprised to see that the voice came from a squirrel.

Except that it was giant. A pile of nuts glowed at his feet.

I struggled to rise, my whole body aching. "Um, hi."

"Hi?" the squirrel demanded. "Is that how you greet the great Ratatoskr?"

His tail fluffed up behind him, a clear sign of offense.

"I'm sorry, your…" My mind raced. "Your Royal Rodentness."

Ratatoskr nodded, his long teeth glinting in the light. "That's better. Now I ask again, what are you doing in *my* tree?"

I didn't mention that this was the world tree, technically belonging to the whole world. Cade, wisely, kept his mouth shut, too.

"We're trying to get to the realm of the Valkyrie," I said, suddenly realizing that I didn't know *how* we'd get there. Last time, the raven had shown up and given us a ride. I looked up. Yggdrasil rose tall above us, so huge I couldn't comprehend it. We couldn't climb that. I looked back at the squirrel.

But he could.

And I'd bet money the scroll told me to get his help.

"Would you give us a ride up to the next realm?"

Ratatoskr frowned. "What's in it for me?"

"What do you want?"

He tapped his chin with his paw. "Well, I deal in gossip, as you may know."

Right. That's where I'd heard his name before. Ratatoskr climbed up and down the world tree, passing slanderous gossip back and forth between Níðhöggr at the bottom and the eagle at the top.

But the eagle had been at the bottom of the tree!

He was supposed to be at the top.

I grinned. "I might just have some juicy gossip for you."

Ratatoskr's eyes brightened. "Really? About what?" He shook his finger at me. "It had better be good, now."

"Oh, it'll blow your mind."

"What *is* it?" He leaned forward, whiskers twitching.

"Have you been down to the bottom of the tree today?"

"Not in a week, no. It's a long way."

I grinned. "This morning, I saw Níðhöggr and *the eagle* sitting together."

The squirrel reared back. "You didn't!"

"I did. The eagle didn't want to be seen, though. She hopped back behind the snake when she saw me."

"Impossible! The eagle never flies down. *I* pass the gossip down."

"I know. You make them fight, right? Spreading tales between the two."

"Not tales! The truth! Gossip that I believe to be true."

Cade chuckled low in his throat. I tried not to laugh, myself. The squirrel was like an old busybody at church.

"Well, the eagle decided to fly down for herself today. I bet you haven't seen her either."

The truth glinted in his eyes. "Curses! I knew something was afoot." He stomped his big back foot and wrung his paws together. This was definitely juicy gossip—Ratatoskr was eating this up. "I must go investigate! This requires a firsthand look."

"Hang on!" I held out my hands. "You promised! You have to take us up the tree to the next realm."

Ratatoskr scowled.

"You're a gossip, Ratatoskr, but you have honor."

He scowled deeper, his teeth more prominent.

"Take us, or I'll convince Níðhöggr to sue you for slander. That's what the Icelandic poet Snorri Sturluson wrote about you, you know—that you spread slanderous gossip."

"Sue me for slander? What's that?"

"It's really bad. They'll take all your magical nuts." I pointed to the little pile that glowed at his feet.

He gasped. "He wouldn't!"

"He would. I'd help him. So keep your word, and take us up the tree. You're fast. I bet a strong squirrel like you could be back down at the base of the tree to spy on Níðhöggr and the eagle in no time."

He puffed up his chest. "I could. And you're right—my honor depends on it."

"Thank you."

He bowed, then picked up his magical nuts and shoved them into his cheeks. I stifled a chuckle. They glowed inside, making him look a little bit angelic, despite his gossipy hobby. Face puffy, he crouched low so we could climb onto his back.

Cade and I scrambled up. Ratatoskr's fur was warm and coarse. Mayhem hovered at our side, and Ratatoskr took off up the tree trunk, scaling the massive ash tree like a pro.

I clung tightly to his fur, muscles burning. My still-healing cuts didn't help matters, either.

"There's no way in hell I'm looking down," I muttered.

"I would advise against it," Cade said.

"We're *hiiiigh* up." Ratatoskr's voice was garbled due to the nuts. "If you fall...splat!"

"Thanks, Ratatoskr." I buried my face in his fur.

Cade chuckled beside me.

This was going to be a long ride.

~

It felt like hours later that Ratatoskr stopped on a branch. I tumbled off him, aching all over. For a moment, I lay on the bark, staring up at the sky.

Somewhere along the way, Mayhem had disappeared. I hoped that meant we were out of danger.

"This is the level of the realm of the Valkyrie," Ratatoskr said. "My honor is intact. Now I am off to determine the truth of your words!"

I leaned up to say goodbye, but he was already scampering off, his bushy tail disappearing over the edge of the branch.

I struggled to my feet to join Cade.

"Never thought I'd ride a giant squirrel," Cade said.

"Life comes at you fast."

"That it does." He turned and started toward the trunk of the tree.

I followed.

It quickly became evident that the entrance to the Valkyrie realm wasn't in the trunk, as the entrance to the Dark Elves world had been. I pulled the compass stone from my pocket and stared at it.

When the needle stopped spinning, it pointed out into thin air, right over the edge of the tree limb.

I dropped my head back and groaned. "You have to be kidding."

"Over the edge?" Cade asked.

"According to this thing."

I walked toward the edge of the limb, which took a solid ten minutes since the thing was so big. Carefully, I leaned over.

Below, the air shimmered black.

A portal.

"We have to jump into it." My stomach turned at the thought.

"And if we're wrong?"

"Splat." I shook my head. "Just like Ratatoskr said."

"That's bad news."

I dug into my bag for the scroll, then unfurled it and searched for confirmation that I should jump off the tallest tree in the universe. "Yep, the scroll confirms that we have to jump."

I shoved it back in my bag, and the stone went into my pocket for easy access.

Cade held out his hand.

I smiled at him, knowing my grin had a slightly worried tinge to it, and gripped his hand. His warmth and strength sent a shot of comfort through me, one that was followed quickly by a shiver.

In the middle of a quest, it'd be a bad idea to think about how attractive Cade was. About how much I wanted him.

But if I had to jump off a giant tree, I was going to take whatever distraction I could get.

"Ready?" Cade asked.

"Oh yeah. Psyched."

He chuckled. Then stepped forward.

I counted down. On three, we leapt off the tree. My stomach jumped into my throat as I fell, wind whistling in my hair. I barely managed to bite back a scream.

When the portal sucked us in, we slowed abruptly, then crashed to the ground.

Sprawled on soft grass, I shook my head to regain my vision.

"You all right?" Cade asked.

"Yeah." I sat up next to him.

All around us, mountains soared, their peaks tipped white. The valley was covered in green grass, with a large river roaring nearby. Wildflowers speckled the ground, and the sun shone brightly in the clear blue sky.

"Whoa," I breathed.

"Looks like Norway in the spring."

"Never been." But now I wanted to. I stood, my legs shaking and muscles aching. "I really hope we don't have to fight anything here. I'm just about out of juice."

Cade wrapped an arm around my waist, supporting me. I stiffened, not liking the insinuation that I wasn't tough enough to stand on my own. Then I relaxed.

I actually liked leaning into Cade. And I liked *him*.

What was the big deal if I accepted a little help?

Especially from him.

I leaned into him and dug the stone from my pocket. The needle spun, finally pointing us down the valley.

"That way."

We started walking. Every step was pain.

When the sound of hoofbeats broke the quiet, I stiffened and turned.

Two white horses galloped up to us, each without a rider. Silver wings flared off their back, and they wore matching silver leather saddles and bridles. When they stopped in front of us, they whinnied.

I held out a hand, and one snuffled my palm.

"Hi, guys," I said.

Both horses bent their heads and their front knees, a clear gesture that we should get on.

"Should we?" Cade asked.

"Yes." I felt it in my chest. We were almost there, and I'd read about the mounts of the Valkyrie. "I'm not much of a horse rider, but these guys will take us where we want to go."

I climbed onto the nearest horse. It was a bit awkward to get around the wings, but I managed. As soon as I was seated, the horse took off, trotting down the valley. At least it didn't fly. I didn't know what to do with the reins or my feet, but as long as we weren't in the air, this ride couldn't go too terribly wrong.

The horse seemed to know where it was going, and it carried me in the direction the compass stone had been pointing.

Cade's mount joined my own, and we trotted down the valley, following the stream. Though I was glad to be going faster, and with an official escort and everything, the bouncing was pretty freaking painful.

Riding sure wasn't easy.

When the buildings came into view ahead, my heart began to thunder.

This was it.

Answers.

The setting sun gleamed on the long, low buildings. Viking longhouses, built of wood with green turf roofs. They were scattered all over the valley. As we neared, I noticed a training field where Valkyrie fought with various weapons.

The women were everywhere. All of them had wings, and most wore armor. Some rode horses like my own, while others fought with axe or sword.

We were only a hundred yards away when one of them peeled off from the group, directing her mount toward us. The horse's coat gleamed black, while her wings shined gold. Chainmail protected the Valkyrie to the knees, and a metal helmet concealed most of her blond hair. Her wings were gold like those of her horse.

A huge grin split her face when she was close enough to make out my features.

"Bree Blackwood! Finally. We have waited for you for ages."

My heart thundered, a thousand emotions battling inside me. Someone as powerful as this Valkyrie had waited for *me*? It made sense, I supposed, since the gods had given me pieces of their power. But it didn't feel like *I* should be that person.

But I was.

Now I just had to earn it.

"Hi." I waved.

Ah, crap. I should have said something more formal.

The Valkyrie nodded, then looked to Cade.

He briefly bowed his head. "I am Cade."

"Belatucadros," the Valkyrie said.

He winced at the use of his true, godly name. "Aye."

She smiled. "I am Sigrún. Come. You must be famished and in need of rest." Her gaze traveled over our blood-soaked clothes. "And a bath."

"That would be amazing." I directed my horse to walk alongside hers. Actually, who was I kidding? My horse did that all on its own.

"Was your journey difficult?" Sigrún asked.

"Moderate," I said.

"I suppose you have many questions."

"That's the truth." I studied the many longhouses and the women who moved between them. Most had stopped their training for the evening. "This isn't quite what I expected, given what I read about the Valkyrie. Don't you live at Valhalla, serving the warriors mead?"

Sigrún threw her head back and laughed. "They would wish it were so."

I grinned. "Good. That sounded crap to me anyway."

"I agree. It is male fantasy, spun by the poets of Midgard." She shook her head, clearly unimpressed. "They would have us strolling the fields of battle amongst the slain, wearing white dresses and choosing the most valiant and serving them mead for eternity. *No.* We do choose the most valiant—or we did. But we rode our war horses into battle, fighting alongside them. Ensuring that our choices went to Valhalla—no matter what it took."

"What do you do now that there are no more Viking warriors or wars?"

"We fight on the front lines of Hel, holding back the monsters who would try to escape and incite Ragnarok."

"The end of the world." I'd read about it.

"Precisely." She pointed toward the training field, where the last of the warriors were leaving. "We train the new Valkyrie there. Then they go to fight."

"New Valkyrie?"

"Of course." She pointed to a section of houses on the left. I noticed a few men milling about, also dressed in armor and looking battle worn. "That is where the mated Valkyrie live. Sometimes, little Valkyrie are born." She pointed to the other side of the compound, where more longhouses sat. "The unmated Valkyrie live there."

As we rode between the buildings, Valkyrie turned to look at us. They smiled, whispering amongst themselves and pointing.

I felt like a celebrity. It was kinda cool, since these women were total badasses, their armor and wings glinting in the light of the setting sun.

"This place is amazing," I said.

"We like it very much. And we're very glad that you are here. I know that you have many questions, but you should rest first. Gain your strength for the trial ahead."

"Trial?"

"It's not easy to anchor one's magic. DragonGods bear a heavy load." She stopped her mount, and mine halted. She turned to me. "But I know you can manage. You are worthy, Bree Blackwood."

Her dark gaze pinned me, serious. Suddenly, it was hard to breathe. Whether it was the weight of her expectations or the awesome knowledge that this real-life freaking *Valkyrie* believed in me, I couldn't tell. But I managed to draw breath.

"Thank you," I said.

"No, thank you. DragonGods are born for a purpose. You will serve yours, but it won't be easy."

All right, that part made me a little nervous, but I shoved it away and focused on our amazing surroundings. I'd only come here once, and I wanted to take it all in.

Sigrún started her mount again. Cade and I followed. She led us to a longhouse on the outskirts of the village, then dismounted.

"You can spend the night here. Recuperate. In the morning, we will convene with the Council of the Valkyrie, and you will have your answers."

I climbed off—more like slid ungracefully—and followed her into the longhouse. It was warm and cozy inside, a long room with a fire burning in the middle. Wicker walls separated what I assumed to be a sleeping chamber, and a young woman looked up from the hearth.

She smiled. "You're here!"

Sigrún gestured to her. "Bree and Cade, this is Herja. She will help you get settled."

"Hi." I nodded to Herja, then turned to Sigrún. "Thank you again."

"Of course. Now, I must go get out of this armor. It's been a long day. Until tomorrow."

I waved goodbye, then turned to Herja, who was already bustling to the side of the longhouse. Her dress was simple and her dark hair pulled back in a ponytail. Though she wasn't dressed like a warrior, she had the bearing and stride of one. I had a feeling that *everyone* here was a warrior, no matter what their day job was.

"This is amazing," Cade said.

"I know, right?" I couldn't believe I was somehow part of this amazing compound of badass warrior women.

Herja hurried back, her arms loaded with a tray of food. The sight of the roasted meat and bread and wine and some kind of root vegetable made my stomach growl.

"You should eat." Herja's dark eyes gleamed happily. "It is a long journey here from Midgard, I know."

"Thank you." I sat on the bench by the fire, enjoying the

warmth, and dug into the food, filling my bowl with a bit of everything.

"Once you've eaten and drunk, you may follow the path out the back door. It will lead you to your private bathing pond." She grinned. "It's geothermal, so it's warm."

"That sounds amazing." Every inch of me ached. Now that we were away from threats, I could use the last of my power to heal myself and then recoup overnight. But I also needed a bath like nobody's business.

"I will leave you." Herja pointed to the far side of the long-house. "There is more food and mead over there."

We repeated our thanks, and she left.

"Mead?" I sipped from my goblet, then nearly gagged at the heavy, sweet taste and pressed my lips together to keep from spitting it out. "Oh, *that's* mead. Not wine."

"Interesting, isn't it?"

"I'd kill for a cosmo." Hesitantly, I sipped at the weird liquid, growing used to it.

Okay, this wasn't so bad. After a day like today, I'd drink pretty much anything.

The sudden quiet and comfort was nice. We ate in companionable silence, both too hungry to talk. The food was savory and delicious, and the mead quickly went to my head. I set down my silver cup and plate, not wanting to overdo it.

"I'm ready for that bath." I stood.

"You go first."

"Come on, there may be two places to bathe."

Cade hesitated for the briefest moment, then nodded and stood. We left the longhouse, stepping into the cool night, and walked down the path. Trees dotted the way, providing shelter from the view of the village.

When I reached the bathing area, I gasped. Moonlight glittered on a steaming natural pool, set right in the middle of the trees. Towels sat on a large rock, along with folded piles of clothes. I inspected them, realizing that they were replicas of what we wore.

I turned to Cade. "This is too cool."

"Aye." He nodded to the pool. "You can go first."

"It's fine. There's enough steam that we won't be able to see each other."

I almost slapped my hand over my mouth. Had I really just said that? Suggested that we get in the pool together? *Naked?*

CHAPTER SEVEN

"That sounds a bit dangerous."

"Don't worry about me, Cade. I know how to say no."

A devastatingly sexy smile stretched across his face. "All right, then. You get in first."

He turned his back.

Quickly, I stripped out of my clothes. My cuts still burned, so I took a few moments to envision them closing. My healing magic surged, and the wounds knit themselves fully back together.

I slipped into the water, groaning at the welcome heat that relaxed my muscles, then looked down. Yep, the steam and darkness concealed anything interesting.

I turned away from Cade. "You can get in."

I heard a rustle of clothing, then a splash. Heat flooded me.

Okay, maybe this had been more the mead talking than me. Because suddenly, this was actually super intimate. I could imagine Cade so clearly, even though I hadn't turned around.

But I *had* to turn around.

Right?

I did.

For a moment, I couldn't see him. Then his head broke the surface of the water and he rose. His dark hair was slicked back from his face, and most of the blood was gone. Moonlight gleamed on his skin, and I swallowed hard.

Yep. This had been the mead's idea. But I didn't mind.

He pointed to my left. "There's soap there, if you want it."

"Um, yep." I waded over to it, careful to keep only my shoulders visible above the water. I grabbed the soap and began to scrub up, occasionally glancing at Cade, who'd found his own bar of soap.

The trees surrounded us like sentries, the night birds chirping low. Moonlight glittered on the water and on the snow at the peaks of the mountains.

Heat grew inside me as the seconds ticked on. Finally, I was clean. I laid the bar of soap on the rock and turned to Cade. He was all the way over on the other side of the pool.

Suddenly, that was way too far.

I drifted toward him, my body buzzing. His lids dropped just slightly, a hot look that stole my breath.

Part of me thought that I'd just drift closer to get a better look at him. But the other part just kept drifting, until I was so close that I could touch him.

I couldn't resist. I laid my hand on the slick muscles of his chest. Heat seared me.

He groaned low in his throat. "Bree."

"Just a kiss."

"Are you sure?"

I leaned up and kissed him, careful not to touch my body to his. If I did that, this would all be over. I'd lose any sense I had. But it didn't matter that we only touched lips. I could feel every inch of him, like magic.

My head swam as we kissed, his lips moving expertly on mine. When his strong hands came up to grip my waist, I moaned. But he didn't pull me toward him, keeping just enough room between us that the water could swirl. Hot images flashed in my mind—us together, doing everything there was to do.

Finally, I tore away, panting. I was too close to jumping on him, and now wasn't the time. I wasn't ready.

Panting, I looked up at him. The heat in his eyes burned me. "We should stop."

He nodded, then stepped back.

I ached to watch him go, but now was not the time.

I turned so that he could climb out and gave him a few moments to get dressed.

"All clear," he said. "I'll meet you back at the longhouse."

"All right." I watched him walk down the path, then climbed out. The cool air shocked some sense into me, clearing my head.

Yeah, I'd made the right decision.

I scrubbed off with the towel, then dressed in the replica clothes. They felt just like mine, but sparked slightly with magic.

I gathered up the old clothes and towel and headed back down the path. When I reached the longhouse, it was quiet, the fire banked.

"Where're the bedrooms?" I called out.

"There's just the one." Cade stepped out from behind the wicker wall to my left. Shadows cast his face in darkness.

"Big enough for two?" I asked.

"Barely."

"That's fine." We'd slept together before. Though this would be different. This was *after* the time that we'd agreed to see where things would go between us. So that made this very different, indeed.

"I don't mind bunking on the floor," he said.

"No, it's fine." I blushed. "I'd kinda like it. A snuggle might be good."

"Might be?" There was a smile in his voice.

"All right. It would be. Let's go to bed." Although heat burned low in my belly, I was too tired to take this any farther than sleep.

Well, maybe not *too* tired. But almost too tired, and definitely too smart.

I joined him in the dark little room and shucked off my boots, socks, and jeans, then joined him in the bed. I snuggled up to his warmth, sighing at the extreme sense of *rightness* I felt.

This was so good.

"What did you mean about being in a dungeon when you were a kid?" The words popped out of my mouth before I'd even registered them in my brain.

He stiffened slightly, then relaxed. "I said that?"

"Yeah, in the dungeon in Svartálfar. You were clearly really bothered by it. Way more bothered than you are when you fight giant monsters single-handedly."

He squeezed me close. "I prefer the monsters, to be honest."

"Who put you in the dungeon?"

"My family."

I gasped, rearing back and looking up at him. "Why?"

"They were afraid of my magic. We lived in a compound in rural Scotland. Near Inverness, just inside the Cairngorms. It was a group of supernaturals who didn't want to be supernaturals."

"Those exist?"

"Not in great numbers." His voice was grim. "It was like any cult, really. And the beginning of my life was fine. They didn't realize how strong my magic was. My mother thought I was just a shifter like her. Then they realized what I really am."

"So they didn't name you Belatucadros, then?"

"No. That name was given on my ninth birthday, when a seer clarified who I *really* am. About that time, the rest of my powers came in. My wolf grew, my speed increased. I found the shield in a field, waiting for me. I could throw it, and it would return."

"Then what?"

"Then they threw me in the dungeon. I was too strong. I think they harbored some fantasy about bringing someone in to take my magic."

"No!" That was terrible—I'd *felt* that. The Norns had shown me what it was like. "That's the worst thing they could do to you. Like tearing your soul out."

"In their eyes, I was already the worst thing."

Tears pricked my eyes. "This is terrible. Did you escape?"

"I did. When I was thirteen, I was strong enough to tear the prison apart with my bare hands. I left that night, and never went back."

"You haven't seen your family since then?"

"Never. There's nothing for me there but pain and misery."

My heart ached, feeling like it was splintering in my chest. I hugged him close, trying to push warmth and caring into him. "I'm glad you left."

"It was the only thing I could do."

"Where'd you go? You were only a boy."

"I joined a band of mercenaries that I met in Edinburgh. We worked together for ten years, all over the world."

"That's how you made your money, Caro said."

"It was lucrative. But some of the jobs were—" I felt him shake his head. "Not for me. So I joined the Protectorate. It's more in line with what I want to do."

"And you've been there ever since. Except for when you go fight in wars on behalf of those who need you. Like a deadly hobby."

"Something like that, aye."

"Why don't you ever talk about it? You do amazing things and never say anything."

"I just help out here and there. It's nothing."

I squeezed him again, liking his modesty.

"What about you?" he said. "Now that I've bared my soul, you can bare yours."

"Nothing to bare." *Kinda a lie.*

And he called me on it. "That's not true. There's sadness in your eyes when you think no one is looking."

"Really?"

"Really. Is it because your sister is missing?"

"Yeah." I sighed. "I miss Rowan."

"And you haven't been able to find any trace of her?"

"No. We spent all our money hunting clues. But we turned up nothing. Just poof! Gone into thin air. She might be dead, but I doubt it. I'd *feel* it, you know?"

Fates, I hope I'd feel it.

He pulled me closer. "I know. And as soon as this is over, and your power is secure, we'll look for her. I'll help you."

Tears smarted my eyes. "Thank you."

He pressed a kiss to the top of my head. "Of course."

I snuggled into him, absorbing his warmth as thoughts of Rowan flashed in my mind's eye. She was all I could see as I fell asleep, and I prayed to fate that maybe this time, with Cade's help, we'd find her.

~

The next morning, a shrieking sound woke me.

I lurched up in bed, gasping. "What's that?"

"Roosters." Cade groaned. "Haven't heard roosters in years."

I blinked blearily, finally able to place the weird noise that I'd only ever heard on TV. I flopped back onto the mattress. "Man, that's a pain."

Cade chuckled, then rolled out of bed. I followed, excitement finally hitting me.

I was going to learn to anchor my powers. To keep my magic. The crazy haywire crap that had been going on was finally going to stop.

Quickly, I tugged on my clothes and boots, then turned to Cade. He was dressed, looking clean and rested and handsome. "Ready?"

"More importantly, are you?"

"Born ready. Let's go." I was excited to see the Valkyrie again. They were so damned cool.

We went out into the living space and found the fire stoked and a kettle of porridge hanging over it. I scarfed mine down, following it with water and wishing for coffee. Apparently the Valkyrie realm wasn't perfect, but I was so excited that I didn't need the caffeine. Sigrún had said that it would be a trial to anchor my magic, but I was ready.

The sun was peeking over the mountains by the time we made it outside. Sigrún waited for us, along with twelve other Valkyrie. They all looked at me with solemn eyes. Their magic radiated from them, strong and fierce. Battle magic. The women wore leather, but no chainmail or helmets. Their hair gleamed all shades, but it was their wings that caught my eye. White, silver, gold, red. They were amazing.

Nerves replaced some of my excitement, but I was still ready.

"Come with us," Sigrún said.

We followed the contingent through the village and deeper into the valley. By the time we stopped at a crystalline pool, I was vibrating with excitement and nerves.

The Valkyrie turned to face me, standing in a semicircle between me and the pool.

Sigrún stepped forward. "You've been chosen as the Valkyrie of the DragonGods. As such, the Viking gods have each given you a bit of their power. But this does not come without a price. You must anchor those gifts within you, or they will devour each other."

I nodded.

"We Valkyrie have the key to anchoring your power, but you must earn it." She turned and pointed to the pool. "Enter the Well of Power and complete the test. Face your fears and unite the magic inside of you."

I swallowed hard and nodded. I wasn't a great swimmer, and I had no idea what the test would be.

But I was no quitter.

I stepped forward. As I passed, Sigrún leaned in and whispered, "Your weakness is that you jump too quickly. Learn restraint. It will save that which you love most."

Her words reminded me of what Jude had said. I nodded, then kept walking.

The water was cold and brisk. I could see straight through to the pale gray rocks on the bottom. I went farther, wondering what the hell was going to happen when I got deep enough that I couldn't breathe.

When the water was up to my neck and no one spoke, I sucked in a breath and kept walking. This was crazy, but everything else had been pretty damned crazy as well. And I could swim to the surface if I didn't like what I found underwater.

Right?

By the time the water closed over my head, I was vibrating with tension. My lungs burned. I opened my eyes, surprised to see that nothing was distorted or weird.

Something inside me compelled me to open my mouth and breathe, so I did.

Fresh air flowed into my lungs.

Weird.

I walked deeper into the water, feeling as if I were walking on dry land. Was it my gift over water that allowed this, or the Valkyrie's trial magic?

In the distance, a short white pedestal protruded from the seafloor. I approached it, climbed on, and stood in the middle. I was still a bit confused about what the heck was going to happen, but it felt right.

The first monster appeared with a flash, leaping for me. My heart jumped into my throat, and a scream almost escaped me. A chain tugged it back, stopping it just before its teeth sank into my neck.

Panting, I studied it. The beast was skeletal and stank with evil, even through the water. It lunged and snarled, red eyes gleaming. The chain rattled, looking like it would break. Sweat broke out on my skin.

Then another beast appeared, and another.

All of them leapt for me.

All about to break their chains.

Ice chilled my veins. My muscles ached to jump into action.

This was the *worst*. The waiting was always the worst. They were chained, but the chains were snapping. One link had already broken on the first beast's chain. It held together barely— one rattle and the chain would slip free of the broken link, and the monster would be upon me.

Sweat rolled down my spine—something that should be impossible underwater but wasn't—as I drew in a ragged breath.

I called my sword from the ether, ready to dive off the pedestal. I couldn't take this—couldn't wait any longer.

Something gentle touched my arm. I jumped, about to lash out.

The ghostly figure of Sigrún stood next to me.

Her words flashed in my mind. *Your weakness is that you jump too quickly. Learn restraint. It will save that which you love most.*

She disappeared

Was that what this was about?

I gritted my teeth, eyeing the terrifying beasts that leapt and snarled. More links broke on the chains, snapping on one side of the metal rings. If the beasts let up tension on their lines, their chains would slip free of the broken links.

The desire to jump off the pedestal and fight my attackers was so strong that my muscles cramped and ached. The fear was a sickening acid in my stomach.

Something warm glowed at my side. I looked over. Mayhem fluttered there, pressed against me. Her presence gave me strength, settling my heart a bit. It still felt like it might break my ribs, but at least it wouldn't break out of my chest.

Mayhem shot a blast of fire, then jumped, startled. Still wasn't used to the new dragon magic, it seemed.

Her fire surprised one of the beasts, which shrank backward. The slack loosened his restraint, allowing the chain to slip free of the half broken loop.

A lightning bolt of fear struck me as the monster jumped, hurtling right for me, ready to tear out my throat.

Everything in me screamed to fight. Every muscle and bone and sinew. But I held still, my mind buzzing with fear.

Pain and heat burst at my back, a strange sensation of something exploding out of my shoulder blades. I screamed, instinct propelling me upward.

I shot out of the water like a rocket. Cold air whipped past my hair, my shoulders, my wings.

Wings?!

I looked back, catching sight of massive silver wings spread out behind me. I was a hundred feet up in the air, my wings holding me aloft.

Holy fates.

I had wings.

Valkyrie wings.

My breath caught. I flew high into the sky, gritting my teeth at the pain in my wings but forcing myself to ignore it and fly higher. This was amazing. In my chest, my magic felt more complete, more whole.

I did a loop-de-loop, the land soaring by under me. I caught sight of Cade, his face turned toward the sky and awe in his expression.

I slowed, landing in front of him and the Valkyrie. My wings still hurt like the devil, but hopefully that would go away.

"Well done." Sigrún stepped forward. "You completed the first test."

"I didn't expect to get wings."

"All Valkyrie have wings. Now you have yours. They will help you anchor your power and give you control. But you are not finished yet. There is one last challenge you must complete for the pain in your wings to fade and for you to keep them permanently."

"What is it?"

"You must prove yourself worthy of your wings by using them in battle, and you must do it soon. Else you will lose your wings, and the pain will stay."

I swallowed hard, nerves skating through me. "And I won't be able to control my magic. Eventually I'll lose it, and my soul."

"Precisely."

Panic rose in my chest, but I swallowed hard, trying to force it away. Panic had never gotten me anywhere in life. I could do this —whatever the challenge was, I could do it. "You said I have to use my wings in a battle, fighting for what is right?"

"Yes."

"But do you have any idea what battle?"

"No. Only that you must prove yourself worthy, which is not easy. Facing one's fears is never easy. Mastering one's own weaknesses is even harder."

I stored that tidbit away for later. "I think that maybe I have to fight the Rebel Gods."

Understanding glinted in Sigrún's eyes. "Yes. That is possible. Have they been trying to find you?"

"Yes." Excitement drummed in my chest. I caught Cade's eyes, and he looked keenly interested, as well. "Do you know who they are? They're hunting me and my sister. I know they're dangerous, but I don't know what they want exactly. Or who they are."

Sigrún nodded. "I think this may be how you will get to keep your wings. You must win a victory against them, but it won't be easy. The Rebel Gods are exactly what their name suggests. They are gods from various pantheons who disagree with the other gods' decision to create the DragonGods."

"Why?"

"They're purists. They don't believe that godly magic should be shared with mortals. They want it all for themselves. When the first DragonGods were created thousands of years ago, the Rebel Gods formed their own faction, breaking away from their pantheons. They come from all the ancient religions. Norse, Greek, Hindu, Phoenician, Native American, and many more. They have one goal—to find the DragonGods and steal their power, using it for their own evil deeds."

"And that's why they've hunted us. *They're* the ones my mother was hiding from." A dark desire for vengeance rose in my chest.

They'd killed my mother.

"Exactly. After the last DragonGod died three hundred years ago, they lay low. They have their own magic, but not enough to fuel their work. But when you were born, their purpose was revived."

"What do they do?"

"Their main avenues of interest are murder, enslaving, and kidnapping—all meant to grow their wealth and power. To have influence over the earth and mortals."

I grimaced.

"If you find them and beat them, I believe that will be enough to prove that you are worthy of your wings. But you must use everything at your disposal. You are not just your wings, and it will take everything you've got to beat them."

"Beat them? Like, kill all of them?"

She laughed. "That is impossible. They are as eternal as the gods. But perhaps you can destroy one of their strongholds that exist in the ether. They use halfway points between the godly realms and the earthly one. These are places where they can walk and so can humans. In rare cases, a god may walk the earth, but it takes great power. Strongholds in the ether are the answer to that."

"I've never heard of them," I said. This magic was way above my pay grade.

"They are places that should not exist," she said. "But with great magic, they can be built. From the strongholds, the Rebel Gods send their minions out to do their bidding. If you can destroy one of these places—and the records they contain—then you could save some of the people that they are inevitably trying to hurt. It will set their operation back by months. Maybe years."

"Okay. I can do that." I *wanted* to do that. To put the hurt on these evil jerks."But where do I find a stronghold?"

Sigrún turned to the Valkyrie who stood behind her. "Gunnr, what do you think?"

Gunnr, a Valkyrie with shining red hair, stepped forward. "Our records suggest that there may be an entrance to a Rebel God stronghold in one of the ancient Phoenician cities. Byblos, Carthage, or Tyre, perhaps. It is hard to say where exactly. You may be able to find the entrance in one of those cities, most likely through a temple, as the Rebel Gods are obsessed with being worshiped."

I nodded. "Thank you."

"You must hurry, though," Sigrún said. "Your wings will only become more painful. Eventually, you won't be able to use them at all."

CHAPTER EIGHT

We arrived back on the main lawn at the Protectorate around noon. The sun shined brightly, a beautiful late summer day.

"Thank fates for transportation charms." I stared at the castle, grateful we hadn't had to travel back down the world tree.

"If only we knew where we were going all the time," Cade said.

True. We could only use them when we knew exactly where we were headed. "That's okay. We survived, didn't we?" Delayed excitement thrummed in my chest. "And we got to meet Níðhöggr the serpent, Ratatoskr, the Fire Giants, and even the Valkyrie."

"You haven't been this excited about mythical creatures on our past adventures," he said. "Quetzalcoatl, the giant flying snake at Texochtatlan, didn't suit your tastes?"

"Ha. Definitely not. I suppose it's just that this is *my* history. So now it means something."

He smiled. "Makes sense. Ready to show off your new wings?"

I moved them slightly, then winced.

"Still hurt?" he asked.

"Never stopped. I need to finish the drill and earn them." I tested folding my wings back into my body. Pain shot through them, a weird feeling since it was a body part I'd never had before.

"You aren't going to be able to hide them that way," Cade said.

I frowned. He was right. Hiding them was an issue. I wanted to be able to go out and about in the human realm, after all. Unless I was willing to pretend to be a movie extra at all times, this wasn't good.

I closed my eyes and visualized my wings disappearing into my back, becoming totally invisible to the eye.

"Good job," Cade said.

"They're gone?"

"Aye."

I imagined them flaring out of my back. Magic sparkled across my shoulders.

"They're back," Cade said.

I looked behind me, catching sight of my silver wing feathers wavering in the breeze. "Cool."

"Let's go alert the others."

"Yeah, good idea. I don't want to waste a second." I set off across the lawn, hurrying toward the castle.

A bark sounded from high on the castle roof. I looked up. Mayhem fluttered in the air, the sun glinting on her blue form.

I waved at her. "Hey there!"

She zipped down to me, flying faster than should be possible for such a little dog. But then, who was I to say what was possible for a ghostly PugDragon?

When she arrived, Mayhem butted her head against my arm, then followed us toward the great front door. It swung open, and I stashed my wings, hiding them.

Just as we entered, Florian ran into the great hall, a large book in his hands and his wig slightly askew.

His gaze landed on me and his eyes widened. "Bree! Just the person I wanted to see."

"Good news?" I asked.

"Yes, indeed! I've translated the book of the Rebel Gods."

I grinned. "That's great news."

"Yes, yes. Let's call a meeting. Jude and Hedy will want to be apprised of my progress." He scowled. "And probably that no good Fopdoodle day librarian, Potts."

"Fopdoodle?"

"You think he's more of a saddle-goose?"

"Um..."

"Scobberlotcher?"

"Hmmm..."

"Lubberwort?"

Okay, now he was just naming off old-timer insults. "Definitely a saddle-goose."

"That's what I thought." Florian grinned. "I'll go gather the others. We shall meet in the round room."

The round room again? Of course it made sense, since this was a matter of vital importance. But still, it emphasized the pressure of the situation.

Cade and I headed for the round room.

"Do you know what a Fopdoodle is?" I asked. "Or a saddle-goose?"

"Not a clue."

"As I thought."

We arrived at the round room just as Jude and Hedy did.

"Florian is fast," I said.

Florian appeared in the doorway at that moment. "Of course I'm fast. Centuries as a ghost.... Do you not expect me to learn the quickest ways around this place?"

I grinned at him.

Jude met my gaze. "Did you succeed?"

"Mostly. There's still work to be done, but I'm on the right track."

The five of us took our seats around the circular table as Ana hurried in, followed by Caro, Ali, and Haris.

Ana ran toward me and threw her arms around me. I winced, pain streaking through my shoulders. It seemed that even though my wings were stored away, they still hurt.

She pulled away and frowned at me. "Are you okay?"

"Fine, fine." *Mostly.*

"Caro, Ali, and Haris, what are you doing here?" Jude asked. "Shouldn't you be on a case?"

"Lunch break," Caro said.

"We want to know what's up with Bree." Ali nodded toward me.

"Personal interest," Haris said.

Jude nodded. "All right. You may sit."

They grinned at me and sat. Ana took the seat next to me.

Jude leaned forward. "What did you discover? Are your powers anchored within you? Do you have control?"

I sucked in a steady breath, realizing for the first time that the magic in my chest felt more secure. More stable. It was like something had been missing, but now it was there. I'd been so distracted by my wings—and the new ache of them—that I hadn't felt it.

"Yes," I said. "I do have more control. Not sure how much yet, but I'm on the path to figuring this out."

"How?" Hedy asked. "What helped you anchor your power?"

I pushed my chair back and stood up, then commanded my wings to unfurl.

Everyone gasped, leaning back in their chairs. The awe on their faces made me grin. Okay, this was actually pretty cool.

"You have *wings*?" Ali demanded.

"They're *awesome*." The awe in Ana's voice echoed in the room.

"Quite impressive." Jude nodded.

"A gift from the Valkyrie?" Hedy asked.

"Not a gift," Cade said. "She earned them."

"Of course." Hedy smiled.

"I've almost earned them," I said. "I've completed the first task to actually *get* the wings. Now I have to prove that I deserve them. I have to use them in battle for the greater good, thereby becoming worthy and cementing them to me."

"Did they have any suggestion about what this greater good might be?" Jude asked.

"Yes. I could destroy one of the Rebel Gods' strongholds."

Jude's eyebrows rose. "Impressive. That would put a dent in their operations and potentially save lives if they lose a base to run their operation from. It takes an immense amount of magic to create a stronghold. They won't recover quickly if you destroy one."

Florian leaned forward and put the book on the table. "That's where I come in. I've translated the book. It's in Phoenician. We don't have all of the language—not all of it survived the test of time—but I think I may be able to help you find them."

Excitement thrummed in my chest. I absorbed my wings into my body and sat. "The Valkyrie said that the Rebel Gods likely operate out of a stronghold that is halfway between the godly realms and the early world."

Hedy gasped. "That would take incredible magic."

"They have it," Florian said. "They are rising again, as we know. They've found great magic to jump-start the process."

"From where?" Cade asked.

"I don't know." Florian frowned.

"Where could their stronghold be?" Jude asked.

"The Valkyrie believe that the entrance is through a temple in one of their greatest cities. They suggested Carthage, Byblos, or Tyre, but it may be another entirely."

"The Phoenicians built temples to their gods," Cade said. "If we can determine which god they're particularly obsessed with, that could give us a clue."

Florian leaned forward. "That's where I can help. One name kept appearing in the Rebel Gods' book—the god Melqart. I didn't know why the name kept appearing, but now that you mention this Valkyrie theory about temples and ancient cities, I believe that you will find the entrance to their stronghold through a Temple of Melqart."

"How many temples were built to him?" I asked. "Didn't the Phoenicians create a great sea-trading empire throughout the Mediterranean? There must be dozens of temples, maybe more."

"None that survived," Cade said. "Except for the one at Kart-hadasht."

"Where's that?" I asked, remembering his fondness for history.

"It's located on the south coast of Tunisia, not very far from Carthage, the Phoenicians greatest port city. But Carthage was a human settlement. Thousands of years of habitation have occurred there since the Carthaginian Phoenicians built their temples. They're long gone. But Kart-hadasht was the supernatural city that operated near there. It was on the same shipping line, which was vital to the Phoenicians, but protected from humans. The remains of the city are still there. I think."

"You haven't been?" I asked.

"No, but I have two friends who work in the area. Archaeologists."

"Could they show us where it is?"

"I believe so."

Excitement swelled in my chest like a balloon. "So this is our best bet. We go to Kart-hadasht and find the temple entrance to their stronghold."

"I'm coming," Ana said.

"Me too!" Caro added.

"You're not getting rid of us." Ali leaned forward.

Haris grinned.

I smiled at them. "Thanks, guys."

Having friends—having backup—was awesome.

"Hold on," Jude said. "This is just recon—not the big fight. You know as well as anyone that too many people on recon can blow our cover and lose the info we seek."

"But it could *become* the big fight," Caro said.

"What if Bree needs us?" Ali added.

"Bree is smart enough to bail if it's about to become the big fight," Cade said. "We follow protocol here at the Protectorate— you know that. It saves lives."

Caro huffed, but nodded.

"We'll perform recon," Cade said, taking over as security expert. He looked at Jude. "It's safe to assume that this can count as one of Bree's training tests for the Protectorate?"

A small smile tugged at Jude's mouth. "Bree must do this to keep her wings and her magic. If she can destroy a Rebel God stronghold, then yes, it will count as one of her tests to join the Protectorate."

"Two tests," Hedy said. "It's really only fair. She's proven much more than normal trainees."

Jude gazed at me, eyes sparkling like stars. "Yes, she has."

I shifted, both pleased and embarrassed. "Let's just get through this first. Cade and I will go to Kart-hadasht."

"And me," Ana said. "You're not leaving me behind this time. I've got your back."

I reached for her hand and squeezed, genuinely wanting her to come along.

"That would work," Cade said. "We should keep it small.

Caro frowned, then met my gaze. "We'll be at the big fight."

"Assuming I don't fix this without a big fight," I said.

She grinned. "I have faith in you, but that's a tall order."

"Yeah, don't leave us out of the fun," Ali said.

"Fine, I'll try to save some demons for you." Or whatever we'd face.

"In the event that we must return to the Rebel Gods' stronghold in their halfway realm, you should create a portal at the entrance," Jude said. "I can only imagine it won't be easy to get through Kart-hadasht. Once you've found it, create the portal so that we can access it more easily."

"How do we create a portal?" I asked. "Isn't that difficult magic?"

"Very." Hedy leaned forward. "But I've developed a spell that can create a temporary portal. It will appear in Edinburgh and connect us to wherever you deploy the spell. Only Protectorate members will be able to use it. But be sure not to deploy it within the halfway realm. It's not strong enough to cross realms. Neither are our transport charms."

"We can do that," I said.

"That's settled, then," Cade said. "We should leave soon. I don't know how long it will take to get to Kart-hadasht."

My stomach growled loudly. "I like that plan. Let's get a bite to eat then get out of here."

"Did someone say eat?" Hans bustled into the room. The skinny cook wore his white apron and chef's hat, an affectation he wouldn't let go of. "I heard from Mayhem that our fighters returned from the field and would appreciate a leg of ham."

"Are you sure it wasn't Mayhem who would appreciate a leg of ham?" Cade asked.

Hans chuckled. "I did think that was the case. So I made you sandwiches. And juice. Juice is good for the soul. And coffee. I thought you might need a pick-me-up. This will revive you."

I wouldn't hate a pick-me-up, that was for sure.

He laid a tray laden with sandwiches on the table.

Jude glared at him. "You know you're not supposed to interrupt meetings, Hans."

"Psst." Hans waved a hand at her, clearly unconcerned. "I'm not interrupting. Just delivering sustenance."

I eyed the peanut butter and jelly that I knew he'd made just for me. I grabbed one. "Thanks, Hans. You're the best."

He bowed, then hurried from the room. The first bite of PB&J was divine, reminding me how long it'd been since the breakfast porridge.

"Eat," Jude said. "Then get cleaned up and come to the main entry hall before you go. I'll be sure to get transportation charms for you so that you can get to Tunisia quickly. If you aren't back in twenty-four hours, we'll send backup. Agreed, Cade?"

"Agreed."

I swallowed and nodded. It looked like the adventures would never stop. As long as I earned my wings, that was fine by me.

~

After a quick shower, I changed into my hot weather clothes and met Cade and Ana.

Cade held up a small black stone. "Jude delivered the transportation charms."

"Great." I smiled. "We're headed to Carthage first?"

Cade shook his head. "To a desert settlement in southern Tunisia, where Doug and Veronica live. It's the closest town to Kart-hadasht."

"They're the archaeologists?"

"Aye." Cade held up a transport stone. "Ready?"

Ana and I nodded.

He counted down to one, then hurled the transport stone at the ground. The silvery gray cloud burst up, and we stepped through the cloud.

A moment later, we appeared in a bustling village. The sun beat down harshly, and I was suddenly glad that I'd changed back into my Death Valley clothes. Ana always said it made us look like we were in *Mad Max*, and fortunately, I fit in well in this supernatural village.

"Wow." Ana spun in a circle to take it in.

I followed suit.

We stood in the central square, surrounded on all sides by merchants with their colorful goods laid out on blankets. Ceramics and cloth, spices and fruit. Dozens of people filled the square, all kinds of supernaturals from what I could see. Except for vampires—because boy, would this sun murder them.

I shielded my eyes to check out the three-story buildings surrounding us on all sides. They were nothing like I'd ever seen before. Made of smooth beige adobe, they were all connected as a united fort like apartments. Roofs arched up at the tops, and narrow, open adobe staircases crisscrossed the fronts, going up to each level. Instead of windows, there were huge open doors at each floor, accessed by the narrow stairs.

"This is incredible," I said.

"It is," Cade said. "Come on. Let's see if we can find Doug and Veronica. I wasn't able to get in touch with them, but hopefully they're here."

We followed Cade through the square, dodging the blankets covered with goods.

When we reached one of the buildings, Cade said, "Wait here. I'll check their apartment."

"Sure thing."

He climbed onto the stairs that ran up alongside the front of the building. Could the little adobe stairs support his weight?

They didn't crack, at least.

He poked his head through a door at the top and called out, then waited a moment. After a while, he turned around and came back down.

"Not home," he said. "So they're either out on a job or trying to convince some locals to tell them where the good stuff is."

"That's how archaeologists find things? Just asking around?" Ana asked.

Cade nodded. "A lot of the times, aye."

We followed him down the row of buildings to the other side of the square. He stopped at a narrow staircase that ran all the way up to the third floor. "We'll try the bar up here. Might get lucky."

I followed him up the narrow stairs, which were built right into the front of the building. They didn't pass in front of any apartments, though I was desperate to peek inside and see what they looked like. They sure smelled good, though, with the scent of savory meat and spices spilling from the doors above and below us.

When we entered the dimly lit bar at the top, cool air enveloped me.

"Wow." I blinked, letting my eyes adjust.

"Aye, the adobe keeps the interiors cool," Cade said.

I noticed a small bar at the back and tiny round tables throughout the space. A little stage was occupied by a fae playing a stringed instrument I'd never seen before.

"There." Cade pointed to a table in the back corner.

Two people were sitting at it, talking to an older man with white hair and a black felt cap. The two archaeologists looked to be in their early thirties, and both were dressed like Indiana Jones, wearing khaki and leather.

I grinned, suddenly liking them.

The man was tall and broad shouldered, with sandy hair and kind eyes. The woman was nearly as tall, strikingly beautiful with her wild black hair tied back with a colorful scarf.

"If you could get a table and some drinks," Cade said, "I'll get Doug and Veronica."

I nodded, then followed Ana toward the bar.

From behind the counter, a woman with gorgeous blue hair smiled at us, her fangs glinting in the light. "What can I get you?"

"Something local?" Ana asked. "Non-alcoholic."

The woman grinned. "Celestia, then. A popular non-alcoholic beer."

"Sounds good." Actually, it didn't. But it also didn't really matter what we drank.

She was quick with the beers, and fortunately, she took credit cards. It might look like we'd stepped back in time here, but the technology was up to date.

Ana and I carried five beers toward a table against the wall and sat. I sipped mine, and eyed Cade, who was talking to the archaeologists.

A moment later, they left the old man, who was now beaming, and approached.

The woman stopped in front of our table and stuck out her hand. "I'm Veronica. I hear you're nuts."

I grinned and shook her hand. "I've heard that before. I'm Bree. This is Ana."

Ana shook.

"Doug." The man smiled and stuck out his hand. We shook, then everyone sat.

I leaned forward. "So, am I nuts because I want to go to Kart-hadasht or for some other reason?"

"Not sure about any other reasons—maybe you've got them—but Kart-hadasht is a bad idea."

"She means it's a death wish," Doug said.

"So you don't go there?" I asked.

"We're not idiots. We do flyovers with our drones and create 3D maps," Doug said. "Data without the death."

Veronica grinned. "It's our motto."

"Not a bad one, honestly," I said.

"It's not. And if you don't want to die, you won't go to Kart-hadasht." Veronica's dark eyes glinted with warning.

"What's changed?" Cade asked. "Didn't you used to go into the ruins?"

"Once, yeah," Veronica said. "But about four years ago, something shifted. The magic got weird. Buildings started to throw giant bricks at us."

"*Throw* bricks?"

Doug nodded. "There's new magic there—violent magic. I don't know what changed, but it all went south."

"Say we were willing to risk it," Cade said. "Would you take us as close as you can?"

"When?" Veronica asked.

"Now."

"Ha, dream on." She leaned back in her chair.

Doug just laughed. "Now's the worst time to go. We can't transport across the desert because it's protected by enchantments. And it's sandstorm season. You'll drown in the stuff before you make it halfway across."

If transporting didn't work, I hoped our portal would. To my knowledge, portals were a totally different type of magic, so hopefully we'd be in the clear.

"But the sandstorms don't always come, do they?" I asked.

"This time of year, they're frequent enough that we don't cross the desert," Doug said.

"What if I could block the sands?" Ana asked.

"Shield magic?" Veronica said.

Ana nodded.

I couldn't tell what kind of supernatural Veronica was. Or Doug, for that matter. They kept their signatures on the downlow. I'd have to ask Cade.

"We'll pay," I said.

"We're not interested in money," Doug said.

Veronica punched him in the shoulder.

Doug sighed. "Fine. We're not *uninterested*. But it's not what drives us."

"It does buy equipment, though," Veronica said. "And nice hotel rooms on vacation."

Doug smiled. "True." He tapped his chin. "This will be dangerous, but maybe we can cut a deal."

"What kind?"

Doug and Veronica leaned toward each other and shared a few whispers. I tried to eavesdrop, but failed.

Doug pulled away. "Five thousand dollars, a transportation stone so that we can leave once we've delivered you, since the protection charms don't prevent people from leaving the city, and when you're in Kart-hadasht, you take as many photos as you can."

"And measurements," Veronica said.

"Isn't it super dangerous in there?" Ana asked. "Will we have time to take photos?"

"Do your best," Veronica said. "We'd like detail shots. Things we have a harder time getting with the drones."

"I can't guarantee the measurements," I said. "But we can do the photos."

Veronica and Doug nodded.

Veronica stood and looked at her watch. "We'd better get a move on. Sun sets late this time of year, but we still want to get across by dark."

I polished off my beer and stood, joining them.

"Good work," I said to Cade as we followed them out of the bar. "I like them."

"Me too."

Veronica and Doug led us through the market, toward the other end of town. We made a brief stop at their place to pick up some daypacks, then continued on toward a corral containing giant camels on the outskirts of town. The beasts were a very pale pink color, like flamingos.

"Can you ride a camel?" Doug asked.

"Ummm." I shook my head.

"Let's hope you're a fast learner." Veronica smiled and pointed to one of the smaller camels who had long, fluttering eyelashes. "You'll ride Camelia."

"Camelia the camel?"

"Yep." Veronica vaulted over the fence.

We followed.

"Why are they pink?" I asked.

"They're a magical breed." Doug collected saddles from the small man who appeared to work at the corral, and began to saddle the camels.

I shifted the daypack that Veronica had given me on my back and approached Camelia, who fluttered her lashes at me.

"Hey, pretty girl."

She honked, the loudest, craziest noise I'd ever heard, and I leapt backward.

"Ooooh, she likes you!" Veronica said.

"Why does she honk?"

"They were magically crossed with geese." Doug grinned.

"That explains it, because she sounds just like a goose." I climbed onto Camelia, trying to get a feel for riding a camel. It was weird, but at least I didn't fall.

Everyone saddled up, and Doug and Veronica moved their mounts toward us.

"All right," Doug said. "Follow our orders exactly. If I shout in French, repeat what I say. Your camel will know what to do. If I give directions, like 'riders, go left,' then do that."

I gave a thumbs-up.

"Don't screw this up," Veronica said. "Your lives depend on it."

CHAPTER NINE

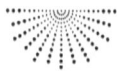

The sun beat hard against my face as we followed Doug and Veronica out into the desert. All around, the sand gleamed in waves of gold, and I felt like I was in *Aladdin*.

"There's a face wrap in your pack if you want it," Veronica said.

As I bounced along on Camelia, I rustled around in the bag, managing to pull the cloth free and wrap my face. Ana and Cade did the same. The ride was bouncy and uncomfortable, but it was better than walking. And flying would just exhaust me. Even now, my wings ached, a constant reminder of what I had to accomplish.

Cade was a natural on his camel, and I stole surreptitious glances at him, unable to help myself. After a couple hours, though, the air started to prickle with danger. It made my skin itch, and I turned around, searching the dunes for oncoming threats.

"It's about to get interesting," Doug said.

I squinted into the distance, realizing that the sand around us was shifting. I squinted at it. A mirage?

I pointed. "Hey, Veronica, what is that?"

Veronica raised her hand to shield her eyes and stared. "Ah, crap. Everyone, get ready to run."

At that moment, the sand exploded about one hundred yards away. A massive scorpion burst free, easily the size of a car. It scuttled toward us, pinchers raised high.

"*Plus rapide!*" Doug shouted. His camel picked up the pace, galloping across the sand.

"*Plus rapide!*" Veronica shouted. Her mount took off, sand kicking up behind.

All right, then. "*Plus rapide!*"

Camelia shot forward like a rocket. I clung to her, bouncing like mad, as she hurtled across the sand. Ana and Cade joined me. The scorpion raced for us, unnaturally fast.

It went right for Veronica, who pulled an evasive maneuver that allowed her to dodge the creature by a hair.

Doug turned around in his saddle and threw out a hand, blasting the scorpion with a cold rush of air. The edges of it chilled my skin, but the core of the blast hit the scorpion. The creature froze up, then fell onto its back.

Nice.

We could handle these scorpions.

Then another shot out of the sand. And another. They raced for us, impossibly fast on their many legs.

Yeah, I'd spoken too soon.

One of them headed straight for me. I could fly away, but I couldn't leave Camelia on her own.

I called my sword from the ether, careful to keep from slicing her, and shouted, "*Plus rapide!*"

Camelia picked up a little burst of speed, and I pulled the reins slightly left.

She snuffled, clearly annoyed that I thought to command her. *As if* she needed help running away from a giant scorpion. She was no dummy.

She raced left, hurtling over the sand as the scorpion gained on us.

More had surged out of the earth, charging my companions as we galloped over the dunes. Ana created a shield to deflect attacking scorpions, while Cade drew his bronze shield and hurled it toward the one that raced after him.

My scorpion was so close that I could hear the snap of its claws.

Ah, crap, I hated bugs.

And this was one big bug.

He was nearly on me now, his tail hovering over my head. I leaned backward and sliced with my sword, aiming for the closest claw. My blade hacked through, but the claw was so big that it didn't make a difference.

The scorpion hissed and waved its tail.

I eyed it as Camelia galloped, raising my sword at the ready. My heart thundered against my ribs.

One shot.

I had one shot.

The tail struck, flying downward.

I sliced my sword, severing the point from the tip. Camelia was just fast enough that she raced away before the blood could splatter me.

But the scorpion didn't slow down. He hissed and raced faster, his tail regenerating.

"*Plus rapide!*" I cried.

She was probably already going as fast as she could, but I couldn't help myself.

We couldn't outrun them. *Should* I jump off so that she could run faster? If my sword couldn't protect her, what good was I?

I tried calling on my sonic boom, but it was gone. Though my other powers were now intact since I had the wings, my sonic boom had disappeared entirely.

"Duck!" Veronica screamed.

I did as she commanded, crouching low on Camelia's back. Veronica hurled a blast of sparkling magic at the monster. As it flew over my head, the sparkles turned to knives.

They sliced through the scorpion, throwing him backward. He tumbled end over end on the sand, the force of the blades driving him away from me.

Camelia honked her delight and raced forward.

All around, the wounded and dismembered scorpions were climbing to their feet, regenerating. They renewed the chase.

"Can't we kill them?" I screamed.

"Nope," Doug yelled. "Just have to hold them off till we reach the Great Drop."

Great Drop?

The sand beneath Camelia's feet began to shift. She stumbled, almost going to her knees. I flew forward, barely managing to hold on as she righted herself and kept running.

The sand shifted again, as if it were starting to drop way.

"*Vole!*" Veronica shouted.

"*Vole!*" cried Doug.

Ana, Cade, and I mimicked them, shouting loudly without any idea what would happen.

Wings burst from Camelia's back, unfurling to massive size. They were bright pink and shimmered in the sun.

Holy fates!

She leapt into the air, her wings carrying us high as the sand beneath dropped away.

I crouched low and hung onto her neck, peering over the side as the sand thrashed like waves below us, deep inside a newly formed crevasse across the desert. The scorpions clicked their claws and waved their tails, but we were far out of reach.

I laughed, the sound loud against the silence of the desert.

We were halfway across the deep, thrashing sea of sand when Camelia began to falter. Her breathing was coming hard and her wings were weaker.

She flew lower, unable to keep herself aloft.

I looked around. My friends' mounts were flagging as well, wings weaker and chests heaving. Crap.

I peered over the edge of Camelia's neck. We were approaching the firmer sand, but would we make it? If we didn't, the roiling sand pit below would devour us.

I was about to jump off when she put on a little burst of speed and hurtled toward solid ground. She caught her footing on the edge, barely reaching safety. I collapsed on her back, panting as my friends landed.

"Woo!" Ana cried.

"Who would have expected flying pink camels?" Cade said.

"Not me." Slowly, I rose.

"Come on," Doug said. "We need to hurry."

Camelia picked up the pace, following Veronica and Doug.

In the distance, the blue sky turned orange. I pointed to it and called, "Is that why we're hurrying?"

"Yeah," Veronica shouted. "Sandstorm."

Damn.

"Get close together," Ana yelled.

"*Assemblez!*" Doug shouted.

The camels, clearly understanding Doug's command, hustled toward each other and grouped up.

"Keep up the pace," Veronica said. "Ana, can you shield us while we're moving?"

"My specialty," Ana said.

The sand whistled on the wind, screaming through the air. The first grains stung my cheeks, and I squinted my eyes.

Ana threw out her hand, and her magic burst forth, creating a barrier between us and the sand. It stopped stinging my cheeks immediately.

"Ride as fast as you can!" Ana said, gripping her mount's reins with one hand.

"*Plus rapide!*" Doug shouted.

We repeated the command, and the camels picked up the pace. Sand battered against Ana's shield as we raced across the dunes. All around, the air turned tan, then red, then dark. It nearly blocked out the sun.

We ran until I thought my legs would fall off from clinging tightly to Camelia. Camel-riding was hard work.

But Ana was in worse shape, sagging over her camel as she fed her magic to her shield.

Around us, the darkness began to lift.

"Almost there!" Veronica shouted.

The sky turned from black to red to tan to gray, and the sand dissipated almost as quickly as it'd come. Once it was gone, Ana dropped her shield. The camels stopped abruptly, panting.

"Cool power," Veronica said to Ana.

"Thanks."

"There's water in your pack, and beer for the camels," Doug said.

"Beer?"

"Only thing they'll drink."

I shrugged and dug into the pack, pulling out a tall can of beer with a label I couldn't read. I popped the top. "Do I just pour it in her mouth?"

"Hold it out. She'll take care of the rest."

I thrust the can toward the camel's head, and she turned, nipping it out of my hand with her big teeth. She held it carefully, then tilted her head back and guzzled it down.

"Nice." I cracked open my water and drained the thing. The water, though warm, tasted like heaven in my parched mouth.

Finished, I grabbed the beer can from Camelia and stashed the empties in the pack. "You know how to party, Camelia."

She honked delightedly, and I suddenly realized where her wings had come from.

"I can definitely hear the goose in her," I said.

"They also have a splash of flamingo, for color," Doug said.

Cool.

"We're nearly there." Veronica pointed ahead. "Just over the ridge."

We started up again, going at a slower pace to accommodate the camels. As we neared the ridge, protective magic seared my skin, sparking and biting.

"I'm not going to like what's on the other side, am I?" I asked.

"Definitely not," Veronica said.

When we reached the ridge, I caught sight of a shimmering wall made of air. Almost a mirage. Danger rolled out from it. Evil. It was a tangible feeling.

I shuddered. The mirage commanded me to go back. Crossing it would be a terrible idea.

"Strong magic," Cade muttered.

Veronica and Doug stopped their mounts. "This is where we leave you. Normally, we'd cross over if we were going to do a job, but since we're not, I have no interest in experiencing my worst nightmares."

"Is that what it does?" Ana asked.

"Yes. Phantom magic, we think."

I shuddered. Besides Del, my friend from Magic's Bend, I'd never met a Phantom I'd want to hang out with. Mostly because they were soulless monsters whose touch made you live out your worst fears. Fortunately, Del was only part Phantom.

"You'll find cameras in your packs," Doug said. "Try not to break them. But if you do, at least save the memory card. Take as many pictures as you can."

"Anything we should be aware of at Kart-hadasht?" Cade asked.

"The ruins are extensive," Veronica said. "It's been nearly three thousand years, but things are in relatively good condition. There's been no human habitation or interference since the city was abandoned at the end of the Phoenician period, but weather has eroded many of the buildings."

"Those buildings did throw massive stone blocks at us last time we were here, however," Doug said. "There are probably more threats as well, but we stopped visiting after the change."

Ana cracked her knuckles. "That's okay. I like a surprise."

I grinned at her, glad to be going up against bad guys together again.

"Thank you," I said. "We appreciate the help."

"Just be careful," Veronica said. "It's rough in there."

I climbed off of Camelia, who honked at me and trotted toward Doug. Cade and Ana climbed off their camels, who went toward the archaeologists like horses who knew they were heading home.

"Good luck." Doug tipped his head, then threw the transportation charm on the ground. Silver smoke burst up, and they disappeared.

I turned to my friends, suddenly feeling really alone in the desert. The sight of Ana reminded me that we'd crossed a dangerous desert many times before. This was nothing new.

"Ready?" I asked.

"Always." Ana turned toward the shimmering wall.

"As fast as you can," Cade said. "Don't stop for anything."

I sucked in a deep breath, then started forward, sprinting with all my might.

As soon as I entered, grief filled my mind. The kind that's as heavy as an anvil and makes you feel like you can't move. Like you never want to move again.

I stumbled, almost going to my knees.

Thoughts of Ana dying flooded my mind. Of Cade. Memories of searching for Rowan through the streets of Death Valley—of finally realizing that she was gone. My mother's death while protecting us from the Rebel Gods.

A sob rose in my throat, but I bit it back.

The images swam in my mind, pulling at my worst fears and memories. Darkness edged in at the corners of my vision.

It took everything I had to claw my way to my feet and keep going, but I forced my muscles to work. I turned my mind toward thoughts of failure—what would happen if I didn't succeed?

The Rebel Gods would catch Ana.

They'd catch me.

We'd never find Rowan.

Failure wasn't an option.

But my legs wouldn't move. The grief and exhaustion had flowed through my body, stiffening my muscles.

No.

I sucked in a ragged breath and called on my wings, forcing them to flare out of my back. Pain bit through my muscles, clearing my mind.

I welcomed it, focusing on the physical pain rather than the mental, and took to the air. It felt like flying through jello, but I kept going. Slowly. Sweating. Aching.

Below, I saw Ana. She was struggling to rise from her knees. I swooped low, awkward in this weird half realm of misery and grief. Her gaze caught on me, filled with tears.

"I thought you were dead!" she cried.

"I'm not." I reached for her hand, tears stinging my own eyes as all the grief I'd ever felt hit me like a ton of bricks.

Her hand gripped mine, clearing my mind briefly, and I pushed my wings to move, cutting through the thick, enchanted air. I pulled Ana's hand, dragging her behind me. She ran, her touch giving me strength. We pulled each other out of the terrible mist and collapsed on the ground on the other side.

I flopped onto my back, crushing my wings, and gasped, trying to catch my breath. The grief had faded, leaving hollowness in its place.

But at least I could move.

I struggled to sit up, and caught sight of Cade collapsed halfway out of the mist.

He hadn't had someone to drag him along.

I scrambled to my feet and limped toward him, tears burning my eyes. When I reached him, I grabbed his hands and pulled. He jerked at my touch, seeming to wake, and surged out of the mist, going to his feet in a lithe motion.

He grabbed me around the waist and pulled me along. We stumbled to a halt about fifteen feet away, panting.

Ana joined us. "That was the worst."

I nodded, still unable to speak, and turned toward the city. The tumbling stone ruins were massive, shrouded in shadow as the sun sank behind the horizon.

"I'll do some recon from the air," I said. "Find out which way to go."

"Good plan," Cade said quietly. "See if you can use your illusion power to conceal yourself. We don't know what's in that city or what's looking out."

"You have illusion power now?" Ana asked. "That's awesome."

"From Loki, I think. But I need more practice."

"Get to it, then." Ana grinned and pointed at the sky.

I unfurled my wings, then called on the trickster's magic, envisioning myself disappearing. It took a moment to locate the gift within my chest. Instead of finding the usual broken magic that was hard to grasp, my different powers felt almost organized inside me. Like I could call on one and it would appear.

A cold shiver raced down my limbs.

Ana gasped. "It worked!"

"Good." I'd need to hurry, though. I could already feel the strain of using the unfamiliar magic. Illusion was particularly draining.

I crouched low, then took off into the air, letting my wings carry me upward. Pain surged, but it was easy to ignore with the wind whipping my hair back from my face and the joy of *flying* shooting through me.

This was totally crazy.

I felt weightless and powerful and...almost invincible.

This was the most incredible magic I'd ever experienced.

Soon, I was high enough to see the whole city, which butted up to the sea. The scent of the ocean washed over me. A broken exterior wall surrounded the city, which gleamed white under the moonlight, tumbled stones from broken buildings dotting the landscape.

Some buildings still had half walls remaining, but others were entirely gone, just leaving a footprint of a stone floor. Those had probably been built of wood, and were long gone. Grass and scrub grew around the stone floor tiles.

A large structure on the far end of the city caught my eye. It was near a harbor, and definitely the largest building there.

Had to be the Temple of Melqart.

Danger radiated on the air, dark spells that commanded us to *go back.*

Well, too bad. There was no way that was going to happen.

CHAPTER TEN

I flew back to the ground, landing pretty gracefully, if I did say so myself.

Quickly, I dropped the illusion, not wanting to waste my magic. "I think the temple is directly on the other side of town. At least, that's the largest building."

"Then let's go," Cade said.

As we approached the city, magic continued to spark from it, threatening and dark. I rubbed my arms.

The exterior town wall was broken and decayed, the earthen bricks more susceptible to damage than the stone of the buildings inside.

"Pictures, guys." I pulled the camera from my pack, and my friends followed suit.

I snapped as many as I could, going for detail.

We passed through the wall, and set off up the street, which was made of large flagstones and bordered on either side by the ruins of old stone buildings. It was hard to shoot photos and stay alert, but I did my best.

Dim blue lights zipped around the fallen stones, and tension pricked the air.

"You feel that?" Ana whispered.

"Yep." I unfurled my wings and called my sword from the ether. I kept shooting photos without looking at the camera, keeping my gaze glued to our surroundings.

Cade called on his own weapons, as did Ana.

"Stay alert for flying debris," Cade said.

We walked by the light of the moon, our footsteps silent. Wind rustled by, carrying the scent of the sea.

"Feels like we're being watched," Ana whispered.

"But there's nothing living here that I can sense." Not that I was some kind of super-sleuth who could smell fresh rabbit poo or hear the chitter of squirrels. I hadn't seen anything from the air, and this place just *felt* dead.

Which meant the ruins themselves were watching us.

How did one fight a building?

"Stow your cameras," Cade said. "It's too dangerous."

I shoved mine in my pack and called my shield from the ether, keeping my gaze alert on our surroundings as my skin prickled.

When the first stone block levitated and shot toward us, I dived, raising my shield. The huge boulder glanced off the metal, the strength of the blow sending vibrations up my arm.

Yeah, one couldn't fight a building.

Hiding and running were the only options. "We have to run for it!"

"Agreed." Cade stashed his sword and shield in the ether. "Fly, Bree."

"I'm not leaving you."

"We can fend for ourselves."

To the left, Ana threw up her shield just as a large rock flew at her. It bounced off her force field.

"Point taken." I took off into the air, my wings carrying me high.

The rocks began to fly in earnest, dislodging themselves from the ground and hurtling through space. It reminded me of the Rebel God woman's magic, but I couldn't feel her power here.

Below, Ana deflected the rocks with her force field, while Cade caught them and hurled them away, darting down the path like he was in some macho video game.

From the corner of my eye, I caught sight of a large gray rock flying toward me.

Crap!

I dived, narrowly avoiding the rock, then darted left to dodge another.

We made our way down the street toward the center of town, Ana blocking, Cade catching, and me dodging.

Pain flared when a jagged piece of rock scraped against my leg. I flew and pivoted, vowing to practice my flying more. By the time the boulders stopped soaring, sweat dotted my brow.

I landed next to Cade and Ana, who leaned against one of the broken walls, catching their breaths.

Ahead of us, the Temple of Melqart rose tall. The top right corner of the austere structure was gone, but the rest looked intact. Several long, shallow steps led up to the square door, and the whole thing was unadorned.

"We made it," Ana said.

I approached the temple, the sense of strong magic increasing. It snapped against my skin and stank of sulfur.

"Almost," I murmured. "Something is coming."

Just as I said it, the ground began to shake. I stiffened briefly, then hurried forward.

"We need to get through that door." I felt it as strongly as I felt the ground beneath my feet.

Cade and Ana raced forward to join me.

A figure appeared on the steps, massive and cloaked in black. Magic rolled out from him, strong and deadly. It was a punch to the gut and felt cold beneath my fingertips. He was still a hundred yards away, but I could feel his magic as if he were standing right next to me.

He raised his arms, his black cloak whipping in the wind, and roared, "I am Orcus, and you shall not pass!"

His voice vibrated through me, and I shuddered.

"A god of death," Cade said. "Roman."

"So they hired him to protect the entrance to their stronghold," I said.

"Worse." Cade frowned. "He joined voluntarily, I would assume. For the cause."

"Damn," Ana said. "It's so much harder to fight people who believe in what they're fighting for."

"Well, they're fighting on the wrong side," I said. "That gives us the advantage. And there's only one of him. Three of us."

Orcus waved his arms, and the earth rumbled again. I wobbled on my feet.

He could create earthquakes?

All around us, the ground burst open. Giant monsters leapt up from the ground, nine feet tall if they were an inch. Shaped roughly like Minotaurs, they also had elephant tusks extending from their mouths. Demons. Inscriptions decorated their tusks, though I couldn't read them.

Ancient monster tattoos?

There were six of them, and they charged as one.

My heart thundered against my ribs as I leapt into the air, letting my wings carry me aloft. It was both a powerful feeling and an awkward one.

I hadn't fought from the sky before, but I was going to need to learn. Fast.

Cade's magic flared to life, stronger than ever before. Because we were fighting another god?

Black smoke rolled out from his feet as he charged toward the nearest demon, and the earth shook with the footfalls of a thousand stallions. It was different than Orcus's power. Visions of battle and blood flashed in front of my face.

Cade meant business.

He hurled his shield at the nearest monster, drawing his sword at the same time. The shield neatly removed the beast's head, but Cade ignored it, going for another Minotaur instead. He leapt into the air to reach the tall creature's neck, catching his shield as he flew.

The beast swiped out with claws, but Cade was too fast, raising his shield to block as he plunged his sword into the demon's heart. The beast roared in rage.

On the other side of the street, Ana hurled her dagger. It sank into the black eye of the nearest beast.

I left her to it—she could handle herself—and swooped low to attack a monster who was glaring up at me, his spear raised to hurl.

He heaved the weapon. I deflected it with my shield, then dived, the wind whipping through my hair. As I neared him, I swung my sword and sliced through his neck, dodging just in time to avoid the spray of blood.

My wings ached, but it worked. I soared into the sky, searching for more prey.

Cade was killing his third, and Ana her second.

There were none left for me. I needed to learn to be quicker with my wings.

Orcus stood on the steps of the temple, rage rolling out from him, vibrating on the air.

Oh, we had him right where we wanted him. With his backup dead, and with Cade at our side, we could defeat a god.

Orcus roared. Lightning cut across the sky, followed by a boom of thunder that shook the feathers on my wings.

Ana lost her balance, stumbling.

The earth must've been shaking.

Which meant—

Two dozen Minotaur monsters leapt from the earth, their elephant tusks gleaming in the moonlight. They were huge—an army of super soldier monsters.

Shit.

There were *plenty* left for me. We couldn't fight this many. Not without some kind of advantage.

Advantage.

The word rang in my head.

I called on my magic, letting it surge through me. It filled me with power, strong and fierce. Joy sang through me.

Yes.

My new wings were amazing, anchoring my magic inside me. I'd do whatever I had to do to earn my wings and keep this power.

I called upon Loki's gift, envisioning myself, Cade, and Ana as invisible. Cold shivered over my skin.

Below, Ana shuddered.

Then disappeared.

Cade followed.

Gone.

"You guys are invisible!" I shouted.

They didn't respond, no doubt trying to conceal their position.

If we'd all drunk the same invisibility potion, we'd be bound by that magic and able to see each other. My illusion didn't seem to work that way, however. It was so real that even *I* couldn't see through it.

A monster roared, then toppled over, a dagger protruding from his eye. The demons began to fall, heads flying off and bloody wounds appearing on their chests.

It happened so fast that I had to assume Cade was using his super speed with deadly results, and Ana was hurling her trusty daggers. I was about to dive and fight, but they were so quick—

and I didn't want to get in the way—that I stayed hovering in the air.

Within a minute, the demons were all dead, their bodies disappearing back to the underworld.

Orcus stood on the steps, rage vibrating from him. The air around him shimmered, and he began to grow. His muscles bulged and rippled as they tore at his cloak. He grew, doubling in size until he dwarfed the large entryway to the temple.

Oh, crap.

CHAPTER ELEVEN

Orcus roared, and my heart beat against my ribs as fear shivered over my skin.

When he swept his hand through the air, and pain blasted through me, I doubled over, my wings losing their grip on the air. Visions of torture flashed through my mind—of me being torn apart by Orcus and consumed. Of Ana being devoured. Cade.

Was that what he'd do to us?

Yes.

I tumbled toward the ground, tears burning my eyes as agony tore through me. I could barely make out Ana, curled up on the ground, and Cade, who had gone to one knee. If I could see them, the pain had made me lose my control over my invisibility illusion.

Oh, this was bad.

I was only ten feet from crashing into the ground by the time my wings caught the air again. I managed to fly upward, wobbling and weak.

I needed to shock Orcus into dropping this torture spell. He couldn't manage it forever or he'd have started with it. It must be costing him.

I envisioned flame ripping through the street, bright and orange. It popped to life, roaring toward him. I avoided Cade and Ana, just in case. I knew it wasn't real flame, but no need to risk it. I still didn't understand the extent of these powers.

Orcus dropped his arms and stepped backward.

Illusion was a much rarer gift than fire. He had no reason to think it wasn't real.

To have any shot at defeating him, we had to attack as one.

As if he'd read my mind, Cade looked skyward and raised a fist, giving the signal for a unilateral attack.

Hey, maybe this fight training stuff with the Protectorate was as handy as Jude always said it was.

As the flames boxed Orcus against the wall of the temple, I flew down toward him, my sword ready. Ana and Cade raced for the wall of flame.

As they neared it, I allowed it to part in one small section. They raced through. Cade leapt high, his sword aiming for Orcus's heart. The evil god swiped out with a large fist, but Cade dodged.

At the same time, I flew for his neck, narrowly avoiding his fist and plunging my blade in deep. Blood spurted.

Ana went for his legs, cutting them out from under him.

Orcus roared, his magic swelling on the air. The pain shot through me again, visions of me being dismembered tearing through my mind. Bile rose in my throat as I faltered, my blade pulling out of his neck. From down below, Ana screamed.

Orcus swayed, then fell, the wounds to his legs, chest, and neck enough to take him down. He fell with a crash, then disappeared in a blast of golden light.

I slammed to the ground, pain shooting through my shoulders and wings.

Ana and Cade were on the ground next to me, struggling to rise.

"Did we get him?" Ana asked.

"Aye," Cade said. "If he survives, it will take him a long time to recover. I believe that golden light meant he was returning to his godly realm."

"Like a super fancy transportation charm?"

"Aye."

Aching, I managed to sit. My wings hurt like the devil. "Let's go. I want to get through this temple before any other monsters show up."

"Agreed. That was enough for tonight," Ana said.

A small smile tugged at my lips, but somehow, I knew this wouldn't be the last of the monsters.

I stood and then turned toward the entrance to the temple. I stepped through, my breath held.

When it didn't suck me through to another realm, my shoulders dropped. "Not a portal."

"Too easy," Cade said.

"True. They wouldn't make it easy for us." Not that those demons had been easy, but still. "And it didn't look like a portal."

I inspected the interior of the huge building. Half the roof was still intact, which was incredible after three thousand years. The floor descended on three large levels, like giant stairs that were only a few feet lower than each other. In the center of the second level, a flame burned.

"The eternal flame," Cade said. "Burned for Melqart."

"Still, after all these years?" I asked.

"Belief is powerful. So is magic."

"Ain't that the truth," Ana said.

I inspected our surroundings, looking for any kind of clue. No fancy carvings or statues of gods here—just austere stone and hard angles. That didn't leave us a lot to work with.

"There are doors down there." Cade started toward them.

We followed, hurrying across the floor. We descended to the middle level and passed by the eternal flame. It drew my eye, but I kept going toward the doors.

When we reached them, we stopped.

There were seven, and each gleamed like a portal.

"This has to be it," Ana said.

"I agree." Cade approached and held out his hand to feel the magical signature. He frowned and withdrew his arm. "But *which* door?"

I approached one, wincing at the prickly feel of the magic. I stopped at each door. They all felt different, but none of them felt welcoming. Not that the proper door would.

"What about the windows above?" Ana pointed to the high windows that sat between each door. "Could the entrance be through one of those?"

"I'll check." I unfurled my wings, taking off into the air.

Every time, flying was a joy. But every time, it hurt.

I flew by each of the windows, holding out my hand. "They all feel terrible. They're portals, too, but none of them is clearly the one we want."

I landed.

"There must be a clue here," Cade said. "Well, if we're lucky, there is."

"Spread out," I said. "Let's find it. I don't want to pick at random. The odds are awful, and those portals feel even worse."

"Agreed." Ana nodded.

We split up, pacing through the building that sparked with magic.

There was nothing on the walls or floor, but the eternal flame drew me toward it.

I stepped to the edge, realizing that the flame burned from a pool of water. The base of the pool was an amazing mosaic. Fire-light glinted off the many colored stones. The designs were strange, almost random.

I squinted at them, turning my head to the side. "Hey, guys, I think I found something."

"Good," Ana said. "Because I've got nothing."

They joined me, leaning over to look into the water.

"What is it?" Kade asked.

I pointed at the weird little shapes made by the tiny tiled stones. "I think those are Phoenician letters. They may be telling us which door to take."

"Can we send a picture to Florian?" Ana asked. "He could interpret it."

"Send it to Caro," I said. "I doubt Florian has a phone. He's not exactly that generation."

Ana grinned, then pulled her cell out of her pocket, started snapping away, and typed out a message.

"There are only two primary shapes," I said. "The triangle and the thing that looks like a bent rake."

"Hopefully Florian will recognize them," Cade said.

Ana's phone dinged and she grinned. "A video call is coming through."

Ana held up her phone so we could see Florian's excited face as he started to speak. "That is most interesting indeed! Normally, simple letters would not be much help. But the letters of the Phoenician alphabet are derived from words."

"Which words are these?" I asked.

"Window and door," Florian said. "The triangle is the door, and the bent rake is the window. So it looks like you have a pattern. You just need to figure out what it is."

My heart sped up. "Thanks, Florian. We can work with that."

Ana hung up.

"Good job recognizing the Phoenician writing," Cade said.

"Thanks." I peered at the letters. "Let's just figure out the pattern."

We circled the fountain, studying the letters. I pointed to one of the triangles that seemed to be out of line compared to the others. It was higher. "That one's different."

Cade squinted at it. "That could be our door. But which one does it represent?"

Ana pointed to a large mosaic flower that sat between the letters. "If we assume that this is the start of the line of doors, the one that we want is the third from the left."

I paced around the fountain to see what she was talking about. It clicked into place. "Yep! I bet that is our door."

"Let's try it, then," Cade said.

We hurried toward the lower level and found the appropriate door. It felt prickly and a bit miserable, like all the rest, but I trusted Ana's judgment.

"Together?" I held out my hands.

Cade took my hand. "We'll have to go in a line."

True. The door wasn't very wide.

He moved to the front. Ana took my hand, and we went through the door. Magic snapped against me like rubber bands, but the door wasn't a portal. We didn't get sucked into the ether and transported through space.

Instead, we stepped out onto the back side of the temple, right where it butted up against the large, man-made harbor. It was square, carved right out of the rock.

"Wow, this is old," I murmured.

"Amazing," Cade said.

Golden light glowed brightly from the door behind us, then lit up the stones at our feet. The shiny glow traveled through the stones on the ground, zipping across and down into the water.

I hurried after it, following it to the edge of the quay. The golden glow sank into the water.

"Weird," I whispered.

I could feel the golden magic in the water. It was like a call. But what was it calling to?

We all peered hard into the glowing water. It took everything I had not to lean too far out and fall in.

When the sea monster leapt from the depths, I screamed and stumbled back. Cade and Ana followed.

I landed on my butt, pain singing through me, then scrambled up. The creature hadn't followed us onto dry land, but a splashing sounded in the harbor.

I called my sword from the ether. Cade and Ana did the same, each reaching for their weapons of choice. Shield for Cade and a sword for Ana. Though she might normally prefer daggers, this beast was big enough to require a sword.

"What is it?" I asked as I approached the edge.

"No idea," Cade said. "Didn't get a good look."

We leaned over, careful not to get too close to the water. A weird animal swam at the surface, head out of the water and eyes keen on us.

"It's a horse with wings," Ana said.

She wasn't wrong. The head was equine and the wings were huge.

"It has a fish's tail, though," I said. The scales gleamed green in the moonlight.

"It's a hippokampoi," Cade said. "Worshiped by the Phoenicians and Greeks alike."

"Cool."

The hippokampoi neighed at us, a weird sound that burbled like a fish but still sounded like a horse.

I reached out a hand. Valkyrie had winged horses. Maybe this winged horse-fish would like me. The golden light had called the hippokampoi to us, so I assumed we needed the creature's help.

It sniffed at my hand, then backed up, shaking its head.

Dang. "If only I had a treat for it. Like Mayhem always has her ham."

Mayhem appeared at my side, an excited gleam in her eye.

"Did she hear you?" Cade asked.

Mayhem gave a little bark in her throat. The ham clutched in her jaws prevented a full bark, fortunately.

"Hey, you have a ham," I said.

She gave me a look that said, "I *always* have a ham."

I held out a hand. "Can I have your ham? I promise I'll get you a bigger one."

She gave me a suspicious look, tilting her head and glaring hard with her left eye.

"I promise." I pointed to the hippokampoi, who was now looking at the ham with interest. "I don't know if winged horse-fishes eat ham, but I need him to be my friend, so I want to try."

Mayhem sighed, then fluttered closer and handed over her ham.

"Thanks, Mayhem."

She barked, a clear, "Keep your promise about that bigger ham, lady."

"I will." I turned to the hippokampoi and held out the ham. "There's only a couple bites out of it. I think you might like it."

The hippokampoi swam forward, sniffing delicately at the ham. Curiosity gleamed in the creature's eyes, then it shook its head and swam backward.

"Dang it."

"Hang on, I think it was interested," Ana said. "Not that I'd expect a horse-fish to like ham, but there's a first time for everything."

"Hmmm." I eyed the hippokampoi. "So this is *almost* to your taste, but not quite?"

"Maybe he doesn't like cold ham," Cade said.

Not a bad point. I turned to Mayhem and held out the ham. "Can you warm this up a bit?"

She nodded, tongue lolling out of her mouth, then breathed a blast of fire at the ham. An image of a dragon flashed briefly over her doggy face, then disappeared.

I rotated the ham so that she could warm it evenly, then withdrew it. "Thanks, Mayhem."

She barked, something that sounded like, "Anytime, pal."

I held out the slightly charred ham to the hippokampoi. The horse lunged for it, chomping it between big white teeth. The creature swallowed it whole, then swam up to the edge of the dock and snuffled my hand. Warm ham breath wafted over me.

"Hi, buddy," I said.

The hippokampoi raised its back. Mayhem barked and flew down to sit on the creature. The horse-fish shook her off, then raised its back again for us.

"I think we're supposed to get on," I said.

"Agreed." Cade frowned. "But aren't we all too big?"

The hippokampoi snorted.

"Doesn't sound like he thinks so." I peered out into the harbor, noticing that the exit shimmered with gray light. I pointed to it. "I think that's the portal to the stronghold in the ether."

"We should deploy Hedy's temporary portal here, then," Cade said. "Last thing we need to do is get into the stronghold and lose our chance."

"Agreed."

Cade pulled a piece of glowing chalk from his pocket, then crouched and drew a large square on the stone. He stood, put the chalk back into his pocket, and withdrew a glowing orange vial of liquid.

"Step back."

We did as he commanded, and he poured the potion over the chalk line. Light burst from the space, and a shimmery orange portal appeared.

"Whoa, cool," Ana said.

"Indeed." Cade stowed the empty glass vial in his pocket. "Leads straight to an alley in Edinburgh, which we've got guards patrolling."

"Nice." I grinned. "Hopefully we'll settle this today and won't have to use the portal, but it's a nice backup."

"This is just recon," Cade said. "We're going to play it safe until we have backup."

I saluted, then turned to the hippokampoi. His scales glinted in the moonlight, and he looked at me with quizzical eyes.

"Ready?" I asked.

He snuffled. I took that to be a yes, and retracted my wings before I sat on the stone ledge. The hippokampoi swam closer. With my breath held, I slipped off the dock and landed on his back.

He was cold and wet beneath me, and my boots dangled in the chilly water. But I didn't mind—not when I was riding a real, live hippokampoi.

I petted his green scales as Cade climbed on behind me, and Ana behind him.

"This is *awesome*," Ana said.

"I know, right?" I gave a little shriek as the hippokampoi took off, much faster than I anticipated.

It zipped through the water toward the harbor exit, leaving a white wake behind it. Water dragged at my boots, and I clung to the hippokampoi's small wings.

Mayhem flew beside us, barking excitedly, little blasts of fire emitting from her mouth.

The hippokampoi snuffled, as if shushing her. She zipped her lip.

At the exit of the harbor, the air shimmered with a faint golden glow. The hippokampoi swam right through, snuffling at the feel of the magic that prickled as we passed. The air was briefly golden and blinding, then we were in a new harbor.

Except, it was full of boats. Big, fat-bottomed vessels that floated, tugging at their lines as the wake from the hippokampoi jostled them.

"Holy crap," Ana murmured. "A real Phoenician city."

"Sort of." The whole place glowed with a strange light, but it definitely looked like an intact Phoenician city. As if the magic had created a place that was a mirror of the ruins on the other side of the portal. But the air felt weird. Almost like jelly or something.

"It's definitely a halfway realm," Cade said. "Feel that in the air?"

"Yeah. I don't like it."

"Neither do I," he said. "It takes great magic to keep a place like this going. Earthly realms and godly realms really exist. These places only exist through magic and spells."

"Well, we're going to find a way to break that spell," I said as the hippokampoi swam up to an open space in the dock between two fat boats. Despite the many boats, the docks were empty due to the late hour. The moon had disappeared behind some clouds, giving us even more cover.

I scrambled off of him, Mayhem at my side.

"Thanks, friend," I said.

The hippokampoi snuffled.

"We'll need a ride out of here," Ana said. "Will you wait? We won't have ham, but we promise to bring you more sometime."

Mayhem gave her a disapproving look.

"Not your ham, Mayhem," I said. "But thank you for sharing."

She nodded in what I assumed she thought was a regal manner. Actually, she almost pulled it off. If she hadn't burped fire at that moment, she might have.

I'd have laughed, except the heavy magic that surrounded this place made me uneasy. Something in it felt almost familiar, but not in a good way.

"Come on," I said. "Let's figure out what's going on and how we can destroy this place."

"How *do* we destroy a place like this?" Ana asked.

"No idea," I said.

"We'll find a way," Cade said.

We hurried toward the long row of buildings that surrounded the harbor. They were completely intact, and I wondered what was inside.

Our footsteps were silent as we made our way past the warehouses. By the time we reached one of the main streets, my mind was buzzing. The magic here was really weird. *So familiar.*

Nope—I didn't like it.

"Pretty empty," Ana murmured.

I nodded, unable to hear or see any signs of life.

"It's not fully inhabited," Cade said. "Places like this rarely are. It's a shadow of the other city because it's easiest for the magic to build the stronghold waypoint after a model of something. But it's not a working city."

"There are people here, though." I caught sight of a light shining from a building that was down one of the cross streets.

I took one last look to make sure the street was clear, then hurried across and headed down a narrower alley. Cade and Ana followed, Mayhem bringing up the rear.

Magic pulled at me, strong and fierce. "We need to find where that magic is coming from."

"Agreed," Cade said.

We hurried through the darkened corridor, careful to keep our footfalls silent. The sense of the strange magic grew stronger as we neared it, welcoming me and warning me away at the same time.

A moment later, we heard footsteps.

Shit.

The last thing we needed was guards on our tail. Especially if they had godly powers. Stealth was our best friend at this point.

I ducked into the nearest door, realizing at the last minute that there was someone inside.

The man looked up from the table at which he sat, his mouth dropping open. He wasn't old—maybe in his forties—and he was built like a bear.

Before he could shout, I lunged for him, knocking him off his chair. We collided in a tangle of limbs on the ground, and I scrambled to hold my hands over his mouth.

Mayhem flew through the room, sniffing the books and

scrolls that lined the wall. This guy was probably some sort of historian or accountant. Those people usually knew all kinds of good stuff.

Maybe this would work in our favor, after all.

Cade and Ana joined me, their eyes wide. The man thrashed beneath me, and I struggled to keep a grip on his mouth so he couldn't shout. Cade hurried to my side and grabbed him, hauling him upright so he could slap a hand over his mouth.

The man reached up and smacked his fist against a silver charm around his neck. Magic flared briefly.

"Crap, I think he's sounded an alarm," I said.

Ana leaned out of the doorway. A second later, she groaned. "Yep. Twenty guys headed our way. And that woman is with them. The freakin' scary one you fought in the Fae realm."

CHAPTER TWELVE

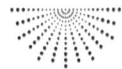

My magic was too depleted to fight twenty. Especially if the oil-slicked woman was with them. She was just too powerful. Cade and Ana looked pretty beat too. And we were on their home turf. If we were going to win this, we needed the element of surprise.

And we'd just lost it.

My gaze shot to Cade.

"Let's get out of here," he said.

"Can you carry him?" I asked.

Cade nodded.

I tore off the bottom of my shirt and tied it around the man's mouth, gagging him. "I'll conceal our escape with illusion, and we'll run for the hippokampoi. Hopefully he can take us all."

"Good plan," Cade said. "Let's go."

"Grab what you can," I told Ana as I snatched up some books and scrolls. The more info we could bring back, the better.

She filled her arms, and we went to the door. I called upon my magic, imagining us becoming invisible. Cade and Ana disappeared, along with our hostage, and we sprinted out of the room.

Our pursuers were still about thirty yards off, thank fates.

We kept our footfalls silent as we sprinted toward the harbor.

Please let Cade and Ana be with me.

When we arrived at the harbor, the hippokampoi was waiting. The guards weren't following, so I dropped the illusion, grateful to see a winded Cade and Ana with me. Mayhem floated at their side.

"Can you take us all?" I asked the hippokampoi.

He gave us a doubtful look, then sidled up to the edge of the quay. We climbed onto his back, the hostage still draped over Cade's shoulder, and the hippokampoi *oofed.*

"Let's go," I whispered.

The hippokampoi took off toward the portal, and I turned around, my heart in my throat. Fortunately, there was no one there.

Thank fates for small favors.

The portal light flashed gold, and we appeared on the other side. Fast as we could, we clambered off the hippokampoi and sprinted through the portal to Edinburgh.

The ether sucked us in and spat us out in an alley. The chill of an Edinburgh evening greeted us, along with a drizzle of rain.

Four Protectorate guards stood there, monitoring the portal. Their faces relaxed when they saw us.

"Thank fates," Ana murmured. "It worked."

"Seriously." I turned to Cade and the guards. "You're sure they can't follow?"

"Hedy blocked it from anyone who means us or the Protectorate harm. We should be good."

"We'll watch it," the burliest guard said. He looked like some type of shifter, and his magic smelled like it, too.

"Thanks." I grinned, then looked at Cade and Ana. "Let's go."

We hurried toward the other portal, the one that went back to the Protectorate castle. Out on the street, a few people gave us strange looks, but no one bothered us.

We stepped through the portal that was tucked into an alcove near the Whisky and Warlock. The ether sucked us in and spat us out in the woods.

"So glad to be back," Ana said.

"I hear you." We followed the path out of the forest, and Mayhem stuck close to my side.

The moon barely peeked out from behind the clouds, shrouding us in gloom. The castle windows gleamed with welcoming light.

The man in Cade's arms thrashed, but Cade kept his grip tight. "Settle down. You're not going anywhere," Cade said.

As we neared the castle, Mayhem began barking, setting up the alarm.

Ruckus and Chaos raced out the main castle door and toward us, barking like mad. A moment later, Jude hurried out after them.

"Let's go." Cade forced the prisoner to walk alongside him.

The man grumbled, but cooperated. Smart guy, since he was totally outnumbered.

Mayhem flew behind him and gave him a little blast of fire on the butt.

"Come on, Mayhem." I shook my finger at her. "Good behavior with the prisoner."

She yipped, then flew away, headed toward the castle, and most likely, another ham.

Jude hurried up, her starry eyes bright in the darkness. "Well? Success? I heard that your portal worked."

"It did," I said. "We made it to the stronghold in the ether and hopefully got some good info."

Her gaze fell to the scrolls in my arm, then flicked to the prisoner. "We can only hope. I'm going to get Hedy so that she can test the prisoner for tracking charms. Then we'll see what he has to say."

"Torture?" Ana's voice wavered.

My stomach pitched.

"No, no." Jude shook her head. "Truth serum. A rare brand that actually works, courtesy of Hedy."

The man began to thrash, trying to pull away from Cade's grip.

Ah, now that was what frightened him. Revealing secrets.

Which meant he had some.

"Calm down," Cade said.

"Pig bastards," the man spat, then he jerked his arm so fiercely that I heard an audible pop come from his shoulder.

I winced.

The man shrieked.

Cade heaved a sigh, then bopped him on the head with his fist. The man crumpled, unconscious.

"That's one way to go about it," Jude said.

"Safest way," Cade said. "For us and him."

Jude nodded, then hurried off toward Hedy's tower, her bathrobe flying in the wind behind her.

Cade bent down and swooped up the man as if he were Fabio and this was the cover of an old romance novel. "Let's head to the dungeon."

We trudged toward the castle, our steps growing slightly slower with every yard. My wings ached, and the rest of me was starting to feel the strain of our adventure.

As we crossed through the main entry foyer, Hans burst out of a hallway, his chef's hat askew and a tray loaded with sandwiches in his arms.

"Mayhem said you were back! You must be hungry."

Cade glanced pointedly at the prisoner he still carried and kept walking. "Thanks, Hans. We will be up in a little while."

"No matter!" Hans said. "I will follow you to the dungeon!"

I grinned, and Hans hurried across the hall. True to his word, he followed us down the hall, sandwich platter in hand.

Hans was always dedicated to feeding people, but this was over the top. Maybe he could sense when people were extra hungry? Or perhaps when they were up against something big?

Because my stomach was growling at the sight of his tray. I didn't know what the sandwiches were, but I didn't care. PB&J, ham and cheese—whatever. I'd eat it.

Cade led us down to the bottom level of the castle, even lower than the armory. It was cool and dark down here, but not totally dank and terrible. As soon as we entered, sconces burst to life on the walls.

We were in a central room that had a table and chairs. Cells surrounded it, their heavy wooden doors looking ominous.

"This place is creepy," Ana said.

Hans set his tray on the table. "Don't worry. We don't hold prisoners long. Just for questioning, then they go to the Order of the Magica for trial."

"That's a bit better, at least." I walked toward the sandwiches and chose a PB&J.

Cade put the unconscious man in a cell, then joined us. "As soon as Hedy and Jude arrive, we'll interrogate him. We shouldn't keep him here longer than necessary."

Hans nodded, though I wasn't sure if he even heard Cade's words, because he gestured to the sandwiches wildly. "Eat! Eat!"

Cade grinned and took a thick ham sandwich. "Thank you, Hans."

Hans nodded, his gaze turning to me. "You have much ahead of you, from what I hear."

Uh-oh. Had I been right? "Is your newfound interest in shoving food on me because you're worried about me?"

Hans made a face. "Of course not! I am a chef! I like to feed people!"

"Hmmm." I bit into the sandwich, which was, in fairness, the best PB&J I'd ever had. "Well, thank you."

"Do you like it? I used three jams! The combination is what makes it superb." He kissed his fingertips.

"It *is* wonderful," I said.

He nodded, satisfied. "Drink your juice. Then interrogate the man and get him out of here."

I saluted.

Cade grinned.

Ana waved.

And Hans hurried up the stairs, straightening his chef's hat as he went. Jude and Hedy arrived just a second later. Caro, Ali, and Haris trailed in after them, all of them dressed in PJs. Ali and Haris wore the footie kind—Ali was a dinosaur and Haris was a turtle.

I stifled a laugh at the sight of the deadly Djinn.

Haris raised a brow at me.

I pressed my lips together.

"Cleary you're up against something big, Bree," Jude said. "Hans has a nose for it."

"That's what I thought might be happening." He was like a skinny mother hen in a chef's hat.

Caro came to join me, squeezing my hand.

"Where is he?" Hedy's voice was all business, though her silver bathrobe was not. The many pockets bulged, however, so she was clearly armed for duty.

Cade swallowed the last of his sandwich, then started toward the cell. "This way."

Hedy hurried after him, digging into her pocket.

Ana and I took our sandwiches with us as we moved closer to the cell door and watched as Hedy hovered her hands over the man, who was prone on the cot within. He snored as she let her magical stone work, trying to detect any dangerous charms that might be clinging to him.

After a while, she stood, the silver inspecting stone gleaming from her hand. "He's clean, from what I can tell. But I'd get rid of that charm around his neck just to be safe."

Cade reached down and yanked the necklace off the man.

Caro stepped up and took it. "I'll take it to Emily. She can transport it away from here."

She hurried out of the room, and Hedy turned to us. "Want me to wake him?"

"Aye," Cade said.

Hedy pulled two little vials from her pocket. She uncorked the blue one.

"What's that?" I asked.

"Truth potion," Hedy said. "A rare formula that I developed. It actually works. Prevents any clever phrasing that might lead us astray."

"Oh, nice." Not all truth serums could be trusted.

"Yes. And it's best to administer it while the suspect is asleep. That way, there's no nasty struggling." She tilted the vial over the man's open mouth. He sputtered but swallowed, then kept snoring.

"He looks so normal," I muttered. Just a dude—average height, brown hair, plain face. Nothing particularly evil about him.

It made him creepier, actually.

"And next, the smelling salts." Hedy uncorked a small silver vial and held it under the man's nose. He snored, inhaled a big whiff of the stuff, then jerked upright coughing and waving a hand in front of his face.

Then his gaze landed on us, and his eyes widened. He scrambled back on the cot. "Don't hurt me!"

"We're not going to hurt you." Cade walked forward, towering over the man.

He cringed backward, paling. "Then what are you going to do?"

"Question you, then turn you over to the Order of the Magica."

It didn't seem possible, but the man paled even more. "That might be worse."

"Then you shouldn't have sided with an organization full of kidnappers and murderers." Cade crossed his arms over his chest. "This could have all been avoided."

The man spat at him, his face twisted with rage. Cade side-stepped, his unnatural speed helping him avoid the man's spit.

Jude looked at me. "You will question him. It's a normal part of Protectorate procedure, and you should get the practice."

I nodded, then stepped up to join Cade. "Tell us about the Rebel Gods stronghold at Kart-hadasht. What magic keeps it in place?"

"I don't—" The man coughed, his brow wrinkling. "I don't know what—" He coughed again.

"You can't lie or prevaricate," Hedy said. "The words just won't come out. So tell us the truth."

"*Something* makes that realm exist in the middle of nowhere," I said. "It's neither human realm, nor god, but in between. So tell us what keeps it going? Is it the weird magic we felt there? How did the Rebel Gods create it?"

The man snapped his lips shut, his dark eyes flashing at us. I glanced at Hedy.

"Wait for it." She winked. "He'll talk."

I turned back to the man, whose cheeks had blown up like Ratatoskr's when he'd filled them with magical acorns.

"Come on, dude. Spill." I waved my hand in an encouraging motion.

"The magic that powers the stronghold is stored in the middle of town." The words rushed out of him, and his cheeks deflated. "It's powerful magic that the Rebel Gods stole from a powerful being. It fuels the place and keeps it...existing."

"Okay. So we have to destroy the magic," I said. "And that will destroy the town."

He scoffed. "You can't destroy the magic. Not magic like that."

He was right. Almost no one could destroy magic. It just wasn't possible. "What is the magic stored in?"

"A flame in the temple. So if you're thinking of stealing it, think again. You can't. It's *part* of the stronghold itself, and you can't steal fire."

Damn. That could be a problem. Unless we could find someone to transfer the magic...

"What spells keep the stronghold active?" I asked.

"None. Not anymore. Not since they put the magic into the stone that fuels the place and keeps it going."

All right. Then we'd definitely have to get the magic out of that flame.

"What's your role?" I asked. "Why were you in a room full of books and scrolls?"

His cheeks puffed up again as he tried to hold his words back. I tapped my foot, willing to wait. It wouldn't be long, anyway.

Finally, they spewed out of him. "Fine! I'm the accounts manager. I oversee our finances."

So we'd stolen their *accountant*. "Why do the Rebel Gods need money?"

"They don't. Not for themselves. But to keep their operations running, they need cash."

"And what are those operations?"

"All sorts, all over the world. People in desperate situations are more prone to believing in higher powers. Like the Rebel Gods. So they create desperate situations."

"And reap belief from those people," I said. "They just want fame?"

"Fame isn't just fame, to a god. It's *power*. It makes them stronger. It keeps them alive."

Hmmm. Okay, fair. Fighting for your life was a solid motivation. "Tell me more about these desperate situations."

I glanced at Jude, who nodded. This was the info the Protectorate really wanted. With it, they could go in and help these people.

The man's cheeks poofed up again, but finally, he spoke. "There are operations all over the world. Sweatshops in Asia, mining in Africa, slave trade in South America."

I listened as he talked, my stomach turning. I wanted to earn my wings to save my magic and my soul—but *this*. He was describing terrible atrocities. We needed to help these people.

Finally, he slowed to a halt.

I frowned. "The Rebel Gods have been busy. How long has this been going on? In earnest, I mean. These particular operations. I know they were lying low for a long time, their power depleted."

"About five years now. They got a big shot of power, and it helped them jumpstart their operations again. They're smart, and fast."

"Are there any more records of these activities besides your office at the stronghold?" I asked. We'd want to get every record so we could put a stop to the Rebel Gods' bullshit.

"I have most of them. There's also the command center, to the left of the temple. There should be records there, too."

I looked at Jude. "That enough?"

She nodded, her starry eyes serious. She turned to Ali and Haris, who stood in the doorway. "Take him up onto the lawn and call the Order. Tell them to pick him up ASAP."

Ali and Haris nodded, then hurried into the room and hoisted the guy up by the arms.

"You can't send me there!" he cried.

"You just described over a dozen torturous deeds you've helped the Rebel Gods commit against humans," I said. "Sweatshops, slavery, murder. You think we're not going to turn you over to the law?"

"You're lucky we're giving you to the Order," Cade growled.

The man shrank back, and Ali and Haris carried him out.

I turned to Jude, Hedy, Cade, and Ana. "That was helpful."

"It was." Jude frowned. "Except we have no way to siphon that magic from the flame in the stronghold."

"Without that, we can't remove the magic that powers the place," Hedy said. "And we can't destroy it."

Ana caught my gaze.

I nodded at her. "We know someone. Phoenix Knight, in Magic's Bend. She's a Conjurer who can transfer magic from object to object."

Hedy's brows rose. "Really? She must be very powerful."

"To say the least." Nix was a serious badass.

"Will she help you?" Jude asked.

We'd already called in one favor with Nix's friend Cass. She'd helped me find Ricketts's goons. But I could still count on Nix. "I think so. We helped her once, about five years ago."

"Then go ask her." Jude looked at her watch. "It's after three a.m. here. If you take the portal to Magic's Bend, you'll arrive in time to ask them tonight."

Cade looked at me. "Do you need to rest?"

Sure, I was dead tired. But there was no time. "I just need to get cleaned up real quick. Then we'll go."

"Me too," Ana said.

I nodded. Ana had helped Nix, too.

"Ana and Bree, if you'll go to Magic's Bend, I'll stay behind with Jude, and we'll do a briefing of what we found at the stronghold," Cade said. "We need a well-designed attack if we want to destroy the stronghold and get ahold of all their records."

I nodded, relieved. Cade had gone with me to get Cass's help before, but it'd be easier if it were just Ana and me. Cass, Nix, and Del were FireSouls, a forbidden sort of supernatural.

They were so powerful that they didn't have to be very wary anymore, but it was always easier to ask for help when the person you were asking was comfortable. Not bringing the god of war would be better.

~

After the quickest shower in the history of time and a change of clothes, Ana and I met in the main hall. She wore her new brown leather jacket and boots, while I favored black. The cool Scottish weather had totally switched up our usual wardrobe.

"Ready?" she asked.

"Yep."

We crossed the lawn, Mayhem joining us as we hurried across the grass. The ham in her mouth was almost entirely intact, indicating that it was probably her second or third of the evening.

Security ham, I liked to call it. Never leave home without one.

We entered the forest, which was still recovering from last week's terrible spell. The underbrush was dead and the gnarled tree trunks were blackened, but they were slowly recovering. Fairy lights had returned to the forest and seemed to be healing it, so despite the fact that the damage got worse the closer we drew to the portals, I had hope that this place would recover.

We'd even spoken to Jude a couple days ago about eventually re-opening the portal to the Fae realm and helping Rocky and Emrys sort out things with the Vampire Demon Bats.

The portal to Magic's Bend glowed white, and we approached it.

"Age before beauty." Ana gestured to the portal.

I grinned. "I'm only a few hours older, dude."

"Hey, I didn't make the rules."

I laughed and stepped through the portal, out into the alley in the Historic District of Magic's Bend. Ana followed, and we went out onto the main street, where partiers were really starting to get their jam on. All sorts of supernaturals roamed the streets, and no one blinked an eye at Mayhem, who fluttered at my side. A group of girls did coo at her, however.

I couldn't blame them. Mayhem was cute.

I hailed a cab, and we hopped in.

"To Factory Row." I glanced at the clock on the dash. Nine p.m. "Potions & Pastilles."

The cab driver saluted, then peeled away from the curb. We rode in silence to the coffee shop/bar that was run by Nix's friends. We'd probably find them there in the evening, and if we didn't, at least we could ask Connor and Claire, their friends who ran the place.

The cab stopped and Ana paid, then we climbed out, Mayhem fluttering behind us.

As expected, the crowd inside Potions & Pastilles was thick. Through the wide glass windows, warm light glowed from the mason jar lamps hanging from the ceiling, and local artwork covered the wooden walls. In the corner, Nix, Cass, and Del sat in their usual chairs.

"It seems things don't change," Ana said.

"Fortunate for us." I crossed the sidewalk and pulled open the door. Music flowed out.

From behind the bar, a young man with floppy black hair and a band T-shirt waved, then his eyes brightened with recognition. Connor.

I smiled and waved, then turned and headed toward Cass, Nix, and Del. They were three of the most powerful supernaturals I'd ever met. Cass, with her red hair gleaming in the light, sat next to Del, a Phantom-FireSoul halfbreed, who had an enormous Hellhound at her feet. Pond Flower, I thought her name was.

Nix, our target, wore one of the funny cartoon cat T-shirts that I remembered. Her eyes brightened when she caught sight of us approaching and she stood. "Bree! Ana!"

Cass and Del smiled and stood.

"Hey." I waved, feeling a bit awkward now. I really should have made a point to visit them more, or keep in touch, if I was going to start making a habit of asking them for help.

"It's been so long." Nix smiled, her green eyes bright. "It's about time you visited."

She sat and gestured for us to take two of the big chairs.

We sat just as Connor showed up. "Long time no see! What can I get for you?"

"Coffee," Ana said.

"Same." Though I was sure Connor could make an amazing pink cocktail, I was too exhausted. It pulled at my bones, so what I really needed was some caffeine.

"With a boost?" Connor asked.

Oh, right. They made magical coffees. "Yes. Extra energy."

"Same," Ana said.

Connor smiled and saluted, then hurried back toward the bar. I turned to Cass, Nix, and Del, but they were watching Mayhem sniff at Pond Flower, who was a massive white and brown spotted hound dog with fiery red eyes.

Finally, Mayhem flew up to Pond Flower's face and shared her ham.

"Nice ghost dog you have there," Nix said.

I thought about mentioning her dragon abilities, but didn't. "Thank you. She's pretty great."

"I'm guessing you need help?" Nix asked.

"How'd you know?"

"You two seem to keep to yourselves unless absolutely necessary," Nix said.

"Ain't that the truth," Cass said.

I blushed, suddenly feeling extra guilty.

Del laughed. "Don't worry about it. We were the same, once."

"Things are changing," I said. "We joined the Undercover Protectorate."

"Wow!" Nix leaned back in her chair. "That's cool."

"Thanks. We like it. But we're in some trouble, and we could use your help."

The three of them leaned forward, interest gleaming in their eyes.

"Is it a fight?" Del asked. "Haven't had a good battle in ages."

"It could be, yeah," I said.

"Probably will be," Ana said.

Del clapped her hands together once. "Hot damn."

"In particular, we need your help, Nix." I explained the situation with the stronghold and the magic that powered it. "So you can see how we'd need you to transfer that magic out of the stone so that the stronghold will be destroyed."

"I could do that," Nix says. "And I've got just the object strong enough to hold the magic. I'll bring it."

"And who runs the stronghold?" Cass asked.

I'd been careful not to give too many details. When I'd seen her last, Cass had recognized that my magic was changing. That I was stronger than normal and something was definitely up.

Since then, I'd learned *way* more.

But should I tell her?

Del, Cass, and Nix looked at me, their gazes serious.

I glanced at Ana, who looked torn. Then she nodded.

I swallowed hard. It was only fair. I hated to share any secrets —but we knew that Cass, Del, and Nix were FireSouls. If they were going to risk their lives for us, they deserved our secrets as well. It was pretty shitty of me to even think of not sharing with them.

And they would keep our secrets. I could count on that.

Connor delivered our drinks at that moment, and I took mine.

"Thanks." I sipped, waiting for him to leave.

Once he was gone and the coast was clear, I lowered my voice so other patrons couldn't hear us. "They are the Rebel Gods, and I am a DragonGod."

All three gasped low.

"Whoa," Cass said.

"Double whoa," Del added.

"Seriously badass." Nix leaned forward. "You just learned this?"

"The transition comes late. I'm the Valkyrie DragonGod, and it's my job to take down the Rebel Gods. This stronghold, at least. After that, we'll see." I *really* didn't like the idea of these bastards running free, terrorizing people. The Valkyrie may have said that it was impossible to get rid of all of them, but I didn't want to believe that.

Nix grinned "Yep. I'm definitely in."

"We were in as soon as you walked in the door," Cass said. "But this just adds fuel to the fire."

"That's true," Nix said. "But I want a piece of the Rebel Gods. I thought they were gone, but if they're back, then we need to get rid of them."

Del scratched Pond Flower's head as she shared the ham with Mayhem. "Have you been okay, otherwise?" Her eyes turned sad. "I have to assume you never found your sister, since she's not here?"

Pain sliced through my heart. "We haven't, but thank you for trying to help us all those years ago."

After we'd first met them and realized that they were capable of finding almost anything, we'd asked for their help with Rowan. But she'd been impossible to find with their dragon sense—possibly because of a strong concealment charm, possibly because she was dead.

"I'm sorry we couldn't do more," Cass said.

"You tried, and we appreciate it," Ana said.

"Where should we meet for this job?" Nix asked. "And when?"

"Meet in Little Grassmarket Close, in Edinburgh. It's an alleyway in the supernatural part of town. Ten p.m. their time." It'd be fully dark by then, giving us enough cover, and also some time to rest up. "There's a portal in that alley. We'll go to Kart-hadasht, in Tunisia, then cross through another portal into the Rebel Gods' stronghold."

"Sounds like a plan," Nix said. "And you really should visit more often. We'd like to see you."

I smiled. "Thanks. We will."

As soon as I sorted out my magic, we'd make it a point. I needed to quit hiding from life.

CHAPTER THIRTEEN

We returned to the Protectorate as the night started to turn gray with dawn. Ana and I hurried out of the forest. I hesitated at the edge, the cliffs calling me.

I wanted to fly, even though I was exhausted.

"I'll meet you later, okay?" I said.

"Sure."

I gave her a quick hug, then went toward the cliffs.

If I was going to use my wings to fight the final battle, I needed the practice. And frankly, I just wanted to fly.

The ocean waves crashing against the cliffs sounded louder as I approached the edge. I sped up to a run, sprinting toward the edge of the cliffs as I commanded my wings to grow. They ached as they sprouted out of my back, but I felt them flare wide, felt the wind rustle through the feathers.

I sucked in a deep breath and leapt off the edge of the cliff, my heart jumping into my throat. Fear shot through me just before my wings caught the air.

I glided, effortlessly soaring over the waves below.

Joy and strength surged, a strange combination with the pain in my wings. That pain was a constant reminder that I had to succeed at this.

But how?

Was it just winning?

No, it had to be more. Like the Valkyrie had said, I had to earn it. To prove that I was worthy.

And my greatest weakness was jumping too fast. Action before thought.

I winced.

Just like when I'd leapt off that cliff.

I wheeled on the air, joining the white gulls as they cawed and greeted the rising sun.

Your weakness is that you jump too quickly. Learn restraint. It will save that which you love most.

Sigrún's words echoed in my mind. But what did I love most?

Ana. Rowan.

Maybe Cade.

I shook my head.

I didn't love him yet. Not even close. I shoved the thought away, mulling over the fight to come, playing it over in my head. Trying to think of how *I* could help us win. How I could make such a difference that I earned my wings?

And who was that woman? She was a leader in the Rebel Gods. But what religion was she from? Her power was godly, that was for sure.

Could I really take her down?

Eventually, exhaustion pulled too hard at me. I headed back toward the cliff, the onshore wind helping to push me along.

A lone figure stood on the edge, the wind whipping his short hair back from his face.

Cade.

I landed next to him, my cheeks chilled from the wind. He looked tired, his eyes heavy and his hands tucked in his pockets.

"Hey," I said.

"You looked good up there."

"Thanks. Trying to get a handle on these things." I pointed back to the wings.

"Succeed?"

"Maybe. I'm getting more control, but I don't know how I'm going to prove that I'm worthy of these wings." I sighed. "I'm just worried."

"Don't be." He smiled. "You're special, Bree. Not just because you're a DragonGod. You're brave, strong, smart."

I nodded, grateful. Slightly perplexed, too. "I can't be that special, though. You're a god. Not to say you're not special, too, but..."

His gaze softened. "I am one god. *You* have the powers of many gods. You are something rare and more powerful, with the potential to become one of the strongest supernaturals on Earth. Capable of almost any magic."

I swallowed hard, the enormity of that sinking in. "I just have to succeed at the stronghold. Find a way to be worthy and keep my wings."

"You will. You're capable of anything, Bree."

I smiled, warmed by his words.

"Tomorrow, you'll have us by your side. The Protectorate. Me. Your friends from Magic's Bend."

"I like the sound of that." I could do this. No matter what new magic was thrown at me, what challenges—I would succeed. Because I had to.

I'd find a way to be worthy. I wouldn't settle for less.

I couldn't.

I leaned slightly toward him, drawn by his strength and beauty and just because I *liked* him. A lot.

"Do you want to sleep at my place?" I held out my hands. "Just sleep, I mean. Sorry. Not propositioning you."

He grinned, sending heat racing through me. "I wouldn't

mind if you did. But no. I have to go back to my place. Get some clean clothes and pick up some supplies from The Vaults."

"Of course." It was better that way. I really needed to get some solid sleep. "What supplies, though?"

"Comms charms. We'll need them to keep in touch during our operations, and this is a bigger team than normal."

I nodded. "Thank you."

"No need. We'll all play our role, and we're happy to do it. We're a team."

I smiled, then leaned up and pressed a kiss to his cheek. Heat sizzled through me, but I ignored it. Or at least, I tried. Reluctantly, I broke contact and pulled back.

"I'll see you later." I skirted around him and headed toward the castle.

I only looked back once, just in time to see him disappear into the forest, headed toward the portal to Edinburgh. My heart seemed to sigh, just a little, at the sight of him.

My footsteps were heavy as I trudged through the main entry door to the castle.

When I reached my hallway, I saw Caro knocking on the door to my tower.

"Caro, hey."

She turned, her face brightening. "Just the person I was looking for."

"Really?"

"Yep." She thrust out her hand. A thin leather cord dangled from it. "For you."

I approached, taking the cord from her. A shiny black rock hung from the cord. "Thanks. What is it?"

"Good luck charm. I know it's important that you succeed tomorrow. I think this might help."

I smiled, my chest warming. "Thanks, Caro."

"Anytime." She grinned, her platinum hair gleaming in the light.

I hugged her, grateful to have made real friends here. They proved it every day—I belonged.

I'd finally found a place worth fighting for. Ana and I could be happy here. Safe. Now I just needed to make sure we held on to it.

Caro pulled back. "Okay, see ya tomorrow. Get your beauty sleep, because I think this one is going to be a doozy."

I grinned and saluted, then headed up the stairs to my apartment. As soon as I entered, I caught sight of Mayhem flying by, an old piece of pizza in her mouth.

I squinted at it. "Where'd you get that?"

She yipped, a noise of definite denial, even though it didn't answer my question. She spun around in the living room to look at me, stopping in front of the curtains.

"That slice has jalapenos on it. Only I order that kind." I looked at the kitchen. "You flew through the fridge door, didn't you?"

She yipped again—another denial—and shook her head.

I sighed. Her ability to fly through doors and bring corporeal objects had saved my butt in Svartálfar, so I wasn't going to complain.

"Well, enjoy." I headed toward the bedroom, but turned before entering. "Just don't go after my PB&J."

She yipped again, then farted, a little blast of fire emitting from her butt. The curtains lit on fire.

Ah, crap. The perils of owning a PugDragon.

I hurried to the kitchen sink and turned on the tap, then used my magic to direct the water at the small flame. It doused it.

"Just be careful, okay?" I said.

She yipped, a clear promise.

I nodded and turned off the water. Frankly, we both needed to practice our self-control.

∾

That evening, after a long rest, Ana and I met up with Cade, Jude, Caro, Ali, and Haris in the main entry hall.

"Right, let's go," Cade said. "We'll head directly to Edinburgh, where we'll meet Bree's allies. There, we'll have a brief meeting to discuss roles, then it's off to Kart-hadasht."

Jude met everyone's gazes. "Do you all understand that this is one of the most dangerous missions we've yet to undertake? You don't have to participate."

That didn't mean me, obviously, since I'd be totally screwed if I didn't prove myself and earn my wings. But everyone else…

Caro nodded enthusiastically. "I'm in. Bree needs us. And besides, it'll be fun."

Jude arched a brow. "Fun?"

"Dangerous," Caro said. "But fun."

"And what's life without a little pain?" Ali said. "Getting blasted by a fire demon just reminds you that you're alive!"

"I prefer acid myself." Haris grinned.

Jude scowled. "I know you take this seriously, but Bree and Ana are new here. They don't know how strange you are."

Caro, Ali, and Haris sobered, then turned to me.

"We really do take this seriously," Caro said.

I grinned. "I know. And I kind of prefer the levity. Makes things feel less terrifying."

"Right. Let's go," Cade said.

I started toward the main doors.

We walked quickly through the enchanted forest toward the portal to Edinburgh, Mayhem following alongside. Maybe I was being overly optimistic, but the damage from the dark curse seemed to be even more improved since this morning.

One by one, we crossed through the portal into the bustling evening street in Edinburgh. As usual, no one noticed us, since there was a concealment spell on the portal exit. I'd had to ask Caro the other day why we seemed to be able to appear in front of people and they didn't blink.

There was a chilly bite to the morning air as we headed back into Little Grassmarket Close, the alley where we were scheduled to meet Cass, Nix, and Del.

Ten figures waited for us near the glowing orange portal. Four guards from the Protectorate, who were in charge of not letting anyone through to Kart-hadasht, along with Cass, Nix, Del, and three tall, muscular men.

I hadn't seen them in years, but I immediately recognized them as the significant others of my friends. Aidan, Cass's guy, was the Origin, the descendent of the first shifter. Roarke, Del's guy, was the Warden of the Underworld, a dark-haired demon hybrid who was in charge of keeping order in the Underworld. Ares, Nix's guy, was a half vampire, half mage who was one of the rulers of the Vampire realm.

I was glad they'd come to help. They'd make good backup.

Nix stepped forward and waved. "I'm Nix Knight."

Everyone made introductions, then Cade stepped forward. "The plans are simple. We'll go to Kart-hadasht, where we'll then cross through the portal to the stronghold, which is a mirror of the ancient city on earth, but completely intact. Caro, Ali, and Haris will go to the accountant's office to get whatever records they can about the Rebel Gods' operations on Earth. Jude, you'll lead Aidan, Roarke, and Ares toward the second location deeper in the city where we hope we'll find more records. Once you've all completed your tasks, contact us on your comms charms, and then get out of there." He handed around the comms charms he'd gotten last night. "The rest of us—myself, Bree, Ana, Nix, Cass, and Del—will head for the eternal flame in the Temple of Melqart to steal the power that fuels the stronghold in the ether. Once that's done, we'll run for it and get out before the stronghold is destroyed."

"You'll have to exit the way we came in," Jude said. "The harbor at the stronghold should be the last place to be destroyed, as it is linked to the real world. If you're fast, you should make it."

We all nodded, and tied the comms charms around our necks.

"Be ready when we go through the portal," I said. "There could be guards there. We caused a...um, bit of a fuss when we performed recon."

Everyone drew their weapons, an assortment of swords, daggers, and bows. I chose my daggers, since I'd be fighting from the air.

A tornado of gray light formed around Roarke, the Warden of the Underworld, and he shifted into his demon form. His skin turned a dark gray while wings of the same color sprouted from his back. His eyes turned black and his features sharper. Next to him, Ares adopted his vampire form, a bigger, harsher-featured version of himself. Del, the half-Phantom, shimmered and turned a transparent blue. Nothing could hurt her in that form.

I let my wings unfurl. "Everyone ready?"

They all nodded.

I led the way through the orange portal, Mayhem at my side. The ether sucked me in, spitting me out in the harbor at Karthadasht. I shot straight into the air to clear the way at the portal, then wheeled around and looked down, searching for any threats.

There were a dozen demons below, all waiting for us, I had to assume. Each was a hulking demon with pale white skin and huge red horns. I debated shielding us with invisibility, but we could beat them without it. I had to save my power for the big fights.

I hurled my dagger at the closest one. The blade sank into his eye. Blood spurted. The demon next to him shot a blast of blue light at me. I dodged, narrowly avoiding the electric shock.

Cade leapt from the portal next, going straight for a demon on the right. Then Jude, Ana, and the rest. One by one, they broke off and went on the attack.

I aimed for the last demon, but Mayhem got there first, landing a massive blow of fire to his chest. He whirled around, alight, and I threw my dagger at him. It plunged into his neck, and he collapsed backward.

The demons were all down, their bodies disappearing back to their underworlds.

I landed amongst the group. "I don't think any of them had comms charms. Hopefully they didn't set off any alert."

"Fingers crossed," Del said, her face glowing a pale blue. "I prefer stealth."

"We'll likely face more demon guards," I said. "But if we're lucky, the Rebel Gods won't show."

"How are we getting to the stronghold in the ether?" Nix asked.

"We've got a ride." I turned to Cade. "Will you go up and trigger the hippokampoi?"

As Cade ran up the stairs to the temple, Cass looked at me. "A real hippokampoi?"

"If we're lucky."

At that moment, Cade stepped out of the appropriate door from the temple, re-triggering the magic that called our ride. It glowed gold, then the light shot through the stones on the floor and down into the water.

I watched the harbor, my shoulders tense.

Little waves appeared, then a shimmering green horse's head broke the surface. Wings unfurled, and the creature neighed.

"Whoa," Caro said.

The hippokampoi eyed us all, clearly doing some mental math. Cade approached and pulled a ham out of the big bag on his shoulder. The hippokampoi neighed again, then whistled.

Four more hippokampoi appeared, swimming for the dock.

"Oh, thank fates," I murmured. "That'll make things easier."

Cade and Mayhem set up an assembly line, with Mayhem using her fire breath to heat the hams and Cade tossing them to the hippokampoi.

Once they'd all swallowed them whole, they sidled up to the quay.

"All right, everyone," I said. "Get on. They'll take us through the portal. I'm going to use my gift over illusion to conceal us as we arrive in the other realm. I can't keep it up for long, but hopefully it'll give us enough time to take out any guards stationed at the entrance harbor. Once we've taken them out, it's go time."

There was a chorus of nods and agreements, then everyone climbed onto the hippokampoi in groups of two and three.

"This is pretty badass," Del said, her black hair gleaming in the light of the moon.

I had to agree. Riding mythical beasts was high on my list of faves.

Once we were all seated, the animals took off through the water, heading in a line toward the portal.

They swam through, and magic prickled against my skin. The air went bright and golden briefly, and I called upon my gift of illusion, imagining all of us as invisible.

As soon as we arrived in the harbor filled with ancient boats, I leapt off the hippokampoi, my wings unfurling and carrying me high into the air.

I spotted a guard lounging on one of the boats, and drew my dagger from the ether. I hurled it, hitting him in the throat. He gurgled, blood spurting, then keeled over. All around, other guards fell, weapons protruding from their bodies.

The attack was silent, and since I couldn't see any of my friends, it was also very strange. Like a weird plague of mysterious flying weapons.

Soon, all the demon guards were on the ground, their bodies disappearing back to their underworlds. It wouldn't be so easy if we ran into any Rebel Gods, but I was going to take what I could get.

I landed on the stone quay and dropped the illusion. My

friends appeared, scattered all over the quay, retrieving their weapons.

Without speaking, everyone gathered into their assigned teams and headed toward the city. Caro saluted just before she peeled off toward the accountant's office, Ali and Haris in tow.

Jude led Aidan, Roarke, and Ares toward the part of town where we thought the other records would be held. Cade had given her a full rundown of everything we remembered from this place, so hopefully she'd be quick in finding it.

I joined Ana, Cade, Nix, Cass, and Del, then led them around the row of warehouses toward the main part of the city.

I led them in a single file line down the street, following the call of the eternal flame. Its magic was strong, the signature distinct. It was a mirror image of the flame in Kart-hadasht in the real world, and the magic felt exactly the same, drawing me forward. It was like the smell of bacon in the morning—easy to follow.

As agreed upon, we stuck to narrower streets and alleys—the places that were less likely to be inhabited or contain guards. With the city intact, it gave us many places to hide.

"That's a strong magic," Nix murmured from behind me. "And a strange one."

She wasn't wrong. It shivered across my skin, at once familiar and repellent.

The shadows deepened as we entered a narrower alley bordered on both sides by wooden houses. The city streets were quiet this time of night, and it was a bit strange to walk through something so historic.

When the first fireball exploded on the ground in front of me, I jumped.

"From above!" Cade said.

I looked up just as another sailed down, straight for me. I lunged left, but it hit my calf. Pain burned.

From behind me, Ana's magic flared. Her glowing shield

appeared overhead. A fireball slammed into it, sending white stress veins through the shield. I couldn't see where the attacker was hiding exactly, but the fireballs seemed to be coming from only one source.

"I've got this." I sprinted out from under Ana's shield, then called my wings to action. I leapt into the sky, flying toward the roof two stories above.

A demon crouched there, so focused on my friends below that he didn't see me. I drew my dagger from the ether and hurled it. As if he had super senses, he looked up just in time to dodge.

My dagger barely missed him.

He hissed, and threw a fireball at me. I lunged left, the flame barely glancing off my wings. The smell of burnt feathers turned my stomach, but I didn't hesitate, just drew another dagger and threw.

This one sank into his eye.

Blood spurted and he fell backward, crashing onto the roof.

Ew.

As often as I pulled that move, I should've been used to the result. But that one had been particularly squishy.

I left the dagger in his head and flew back to my friends. It'd be gross when I called it back to the ether, but I didn't have time to be persnickety.

I landed with my friends. Ana let her shield drop.

"Nice work," Cass said.

"Thanks." I turned and started down the alley again.

The buildings turned from wood to stone, indicating that we were probably entering a wealthier part of town. Maybe the business district, though I had no idea. Doug and Veronica would have loved this place.

Tension tugged at my muscles as we went. There would be more attacks—there was no way around it. I just wanted them to start already, and save me this suspense.

Eventually, we spilled out into a square. As soon as I stepped over the threshold and out into the alley, magic popped against my skin.

"Oh damn," I murmured.

Next to me, Nix raised her bow and arrow. "Yep. That's gonna be a problem."

Cade joined me, smelling the air just slightly. "Demon beast."

I sniffed, getting a hit of sulfur. I winced.

A roar sounded, deep and bellowing.

Yep. Our cover was shot.

CHAPTER FOURTEEN

A huge monster crashed into the square, breaking down a wooden building to the right. The creature was shaped like a boar but covered in yellow scales. Serrated back tusks extended out from its face, ready to slice.

Next to me, Cade's magic surged. "I'll distract him. You kill."

He shifted into his wolf form, and charged. On my other side, magic swirled around Cass. She, too, turned into a giant wolf, and I recalled that she was a Mirror Mage, someone who was able to mimic another person's magic.

She joined Cade, charging across the courtyard and leaping for the monster's neck. Cade got a bite into the belly of the beast, but it wasn't enough. The creature thrashed, shaking Cass off its neck. Beady black eyes landed on us.

I shot into the sky, drawing my dagger from the ether. I'd have to throw hard and be sure to hit an eye. I flew overtop of the creature and aimed.

Before I could throw, Del ran out into the middle of the courtyard, her Phantom form glowing blue. Her magic surged, and she hurled a massive icicle at the monster.

It plunged through the beast's neck like a harpoon, increasing the damage that Cass had already done. Cade's wolf leapt onto the beast, throwing it to its side. One of Nix's arrows flew through the air, piercing the monster through the eye. She stood on the other side of the courtyard, brown hair blowing in the wind.

I stashed my dagger back in the ether. With friends like these, who needed to fight?

I rejoined my companions on the ground as Cade and Cass shifted back into their human forms.

"Let's get a move on. Reinforcements will probably be coming." In fact, it felt like the magic here had increased, as if maybe more Rebel Gods were showing up already.

That would be bad.

I hurried from the square, heading for an alley. We crossed several streets before coming to an amphitheater on our right. We stood at the top, and the seats stretched down to a stage that butted up to the waveless sea. An eerie silence filled the emptiness.

We were halfway past the amphitheater when Del stopped, shushing us.

We halted dead in our tracks.

"Someone is coming," Del said.

I perked my ears, but heard nothing.

"Super hearing," Cass said.

I nodded. "I'll scout it out. Stay here."

Everyone stood silently as I shot into the air, calling upon my illusion to conceal myself. I stopped about two hundred feet up, surveying the terrain. The city was built on a grid, and at first, I couldn't see the attackers.

Then something moved in the shadows.

A contingent of about thirty demon soldiers was coming our way.

Crap.

Too many.

I searched the city, hoping a solution would hit me. A large fountain spewed water in the center of town, directly in line with the amphitheater and the sea. If the demons kept going the way they were, and turned onto that street….

I flew low and whispered to my friends, "Clear out! Away from this street!"

They hurried out of the way, pressing their backs against the buildings. I shot into the air, spotting the demons as the last one turned onto the desired street.

Jackpot.

I called on my gift over water, reaching for the liquid in the fountain. My power surged immediately, my wings making my gift so much more reliable.

I envisioned thousands of gallons of water shooting up from the ground below, and it did as I commanded. I directed the huge wash of water down the street. It roared and crashed against the building walls, catching up with the soldiers and bowling them over. They shouted and flailed, but the water was too deep and too fast.

More. More!

The water surged, washing them down the street toward the amphitheater. I sent them crashing down the steps, where I commanded a massive wave from the ocean to pick them up off the stage and suck them into the sea.

Power rushed through me, making me feel invincible. I loved having my magic anchored inside me. The control was amazing.

I grinned as the last of the water drained away, and flew back to my friends. I landed quietly.

"Wow, you've really come into your own," Nix said.

"Thanks." It meant a lot, coming from her. The things I'd seen Nix do would blow any supernatural's mind. "Let's go."

"The eternal flame is close," Cade said.

"Good, because I hear more company," Del said.

We spilled out into a courtyard a moment later, right in front of a massive temple that looked just like the one back in Karthadasht.

"The eternal flame is in there." I pointed.

A dozen demons ran out of the temple, weapons raised. Guards.

The ones on the edges threw fireballs. I dived left, narrowly avoiding one. My leg was still burning from where I'd gotten hit earlier, and I was clumsy.

Cade hurled his shield at one of the fire demons, taking its head. Next to me, Nix drew her bow, beginning to fire. Ana threw one of her daggers, and Del raced toward the demons fearlessly, confident in her Phantom form's ability to protect her. Cass shot a lightning bolt and hit a demon square in the chest.

I drew my sword and shield and ran for the nearest demon, stowing my wings away.

The demon was at least eight feet tall, his sword a huge sweep of iron. He swung it as I neared, and I slid low, under the slice of the blade.

I swiped out with my sword, taking out one of his legs with a deep gash.

He roared as I hopped to my feet on the other side of him and thrust my blade into his back. He yanked away, spinning and bringing his blade toward me.

I jumped back, unable to avoid him entirely. His blade sliced against my stomach, sending a shot of pain through me. I gasped, but it wasn't deep.

I ducked low, narrowly avoiding his second stroke, and plunged my blade into his heart.

His eyes widened with shock.

I kicked him in the stomach, dislodging him from my blade.

Pain twisted his features. As he fell, he hissed, "They're coming."

Damn. He had to mean the Rebel Gods.

He crashed to the ground.

I turned, searching the courtyard. The demons were all felled, quickly disappearing back to their underworlds. My friends raced for the temple. I followed, sprinting up the steps.

"The Rebel Gods are coming," I shouted as we entered. "As quick as you can, Nix."

"On it!" She ran for the eternal flame, which burned brightly in the middle of the empty, austere temple.

It emitted a magic that hit me straight in the gut. Memories flitted in my mind, but they were so shadowy that I couldn't place them.

But it was familiar somehow. *Definitely* familiar.

I shook my head and turned from the flame.

"Everyone take your places!" I said.

We split up, each taking a spot in the temple, ready to defend Nix as she worked. I was positioned about ten feet in front of her, next to Ana, who would use her shield to protect her. The others scattered around the temple.

I raised my sword and shield. My wings were unfurled. I could take flight at any moment. Tension sang across my skin as I waited for the Rebel Gods. The guards had called them. They were coming.

But could we fight them?

When a voice crackled out of my comms charm, I nearly jumped out of my skin.

"We've got the documents," Caro said. "We're getting out."

"Hurry," I said, my gaze glued to the door.

Come on. Come on.

I glanced back at Nix. She knelt next to the flame, her hand stretched out and glowing blue. At her side sat an ugly black rock. It was probably the vessel into which she was transferring the magic.

Nix had to hurry, or we'd be in for a real fight. Tension felt like spiders crawling over my skin as I waited, readiness pulling my muscles tight.

"Halfway there!" Nix said. "There's a lot of power here."

I bounced on my feet.

Come on.

Then she stepped through the door. The woman. Again, she was slicked with shiny black oil, her eyes burning bright from within her face. Her magic rolled over me like a wave, sucking the breath from my lungs.

Three Rebel Gods surged into the room behind her. Their magic exploded into the temple, signatures so strong that they made my eyes water. The scent of sulfur, the sounds of screams, the taste of blood.

A huge man who was surrounded by flurries of snow charged Del, who powered up her icicle gift and hurled a huge one at him. He smacked it aside with his hand. It shattered against the wall.

Cade charged a huge god with horns bedecked in gold, while Cass leapt for a goddess who wore a Greek style dress. She dripped blood from her skin, as if she were sweating it.

I took flight, hovering over the woman.

"Hey, you!"

She looked up, green eyes glinting. The black oil that slicked her skin glowed in the light of the eternal flame. Her magic rushed over me like ice. I raised my shield, my heart pounding

She hurled a lightning bolt at me. Thunder cracked in the temple, deafening. My eardrums ached as I dodged, narrowly avoiding the blast. It plowed into the ceiling above, smashing apart the marble, which plummeted.

"Look alive, Ana!" Terrified, I glanced toward Nix and Ana.

The rocks bounced off Ana's shield, and Nix was hard at work, her brow creased.

I turned back to the woman. Mayhem darted around the air, trying to get close enough to blow fire at the woman. But her flame was coming in tiny puffs—she'd used most of it up already.

I threw my dagger. She darted left. I called my other dagger from the ether, throwing it as she heaved another bolt of lightning at me.

I dodged as the lightning cracked toward me.

My dagger's blade sliced through her arm as the lightning bolt hit me in the foot. Pain surged and I tumbled through the air, briefly losing control.

I slammed to the ground, right next to Cass, who was wrestling with the blood-covered god. Mayhem flew circles around me, guarding.

Aching, I scrambled to my feet and took to the air again, hurling another dagger at the woman.

She shrieked and threw another lightning bolt. I dived away, but the ceiling shattered, half of it raining down. I barely managed to avoid being crushed.

The horned Rebel God howled as one of the giant stones landed on his shoulder. It gave Cade the advantage, and he leapt on the god.

"Almost there!" Nix yelled.

"Get her!" shrieked the blood-covered Rebel God.

Below, the woman hurled another bolt of lightning at me. I dodged, easily avoiding it. Had it been weaker?

Was she flagging?

Her shoulders were slightly slumped.

"Closer!" Nix yelled.

We were so close. Where was Jude, though? Had she succeeded? We couldn't finish this before she and the guys were out of here.

My comms charm crackled, and Jude's voice came through, as if she'd heard my thoughts.

"We're done," she said. "You need backup?"

I glanced around quickly. It was a mess, but we seemed to be holding our own. And they needed to get the hell out of here if Nix was almost done. If they didn't make it out before the magic was gone, they could get caught here as the stronghold collapsed in on itself. And the Protectorate needed those records to help the people being tortured by the Rebel Gods.

"No, go!" I shouted. "Get out of here!"

"Roger."

The woman raised her arms, and my stomach dropped. She'd pulled this trick with the rocks last time.

As if on cue, the broken marble from the ceiling rose off the ground. Her green eyes burned as she waved her hands in my direction. The rocks shot toward me, thousands of pounds of stone about to pulverize my bones.

My heart leapt into my chest.

I didn't know if the rocks could hurt Mayhem, but I shouted, "Run, Mayhem!"

The little PugDragon yipped, but stayed flying at my side.

"Finished!" Nix shouted.

The woman sagged. Her rocks dropped to the ground right before they would have hit me.

Fear thundered in my ears.

Was her magic somehow tied to the eternal flame?

I called my dagger from the ether, ready to hurl it while she was down. If she wasn't on her guard, I could hit her.

This was my chance.

I raised my arm, about to throw.

Kill shot.

Time slowed. My friends were still wrestling with the Rebel Gods as thunder began to shake the air. The stronghold was starting to collapse in on itself.

I focused my aim on the woman.

Her shoulders were slumped as she kneeled on the ground.

Something stilled my arm.

Wait.

I hesitated.

This was insane. Why would I wait?

Wait.

Look before you leap.

I lowered the dagger, staring at the woman.

An enormous roar shook the stronghold as Nix ran out of the temple, the rock clutched in her arm. As soon as she crossed the threshold, the black oil slicked away from the woman's face, disappearing down her body.

Confusion fuzzed my mind.

Near her, the horned god seemed to notice that she had changed. He roared, then ran from his fight with Cade and grabbed the woman around the waist, lifting her up.

As he lifted her, I caught sight of her face.

Green eyes turned to blue.

Confusion.

Fear.

Rowan.

CHAPTER FIFTEEN

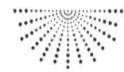

Someone in my mind screamed. Shock chilled my skin.

The woman was *my sister.*

In the flash of an eye, the other Rebel Gods ran from their fights and joined the horned god. I flew toward them, determined to reach Rowan.

But I was too far away.

The horned god threw a stone to the ground, and a blast of golden light plumed upward.

I made eye contact with Rowan as she was dragged into the light by the horned god, transporting away. I reached for her, tears blurring my vision.

Recognition flashed in her eyes, then she was gone.

"No!" I screamed, landing hard on the ground. "Rowan!"

Cade raced to me and grabbed my arm and pulled. "Come on! We have to get out of here."

Del and Cass sprinted out of the temple. The constant roar of the world collapsing was nearly deafening.

That had been Rowan.

Ana ran up to me, tears in her eyes. "I saw her!"

I wasn't crazy.

"Come on!" Cade shouted.

I snapped into action. He was right. Rowan was gone. And we had to get gone, or we'd be crushed within this world.

I sprinted out of the temple, my foot aching from the lightning blow. Cade and Ana ran at my side, Mayhem leading the way. All around, the world was lit with an orange glow. Dust billowed up from all sides, growing closer as the world collapsed from the outside in, toward the harbor in the middle.

I prayed that Jude was right—that the harbor would be the last thing to go because it was connected to the real world.

We raced across the courtyard, but the destruction was too fast. We were too slow.

Ahead of me, light shimmered around Cass as she transformed into a large griffon. The beast had the head of an eagle and the body of a lion. Massive wings flared high. Del and Nix leapt onto her back, and she took off into the air.

Next to me, Cade shifted into his wolf form, then howled. I jumped onto his back, Ana following. We clung to him as he sprinted through the city, his wolf speed blowing my hair back from my face. We raced after Cass, Nix, and Del, keeping up easily. Mayhem raced alongside, her dark eyes wide.

All around, dust billowed up as the destruction neared. Buildings cracked and toppled, and the roar of thunder grew louder.

Would we make it?

Fear chilled my skin as I began to breathe in the dust. It became hard to see.

When we spilled out into the harbor, the sight of the hippokampoi was the most amazing thing I'd ever seen.

Aidan, Roarke, and Ares waited at the edge, their gazes glued to Cass, Nix, and Del. Cass landed, her claws clattering on the stone. Del and Nix leapt off her back and hugged Roarke and Ares.

Cass shifted back to human and yelled, "You shouldn't have waited!"

"Ha!" Aidan climbed onto a hippokampoi. "As if we'd leave."

They all piled onto hippokampoi.

Cade stopped in front of the water, and Ana and I jumped off his back. All around, the world was chaos. Destruction was breathing down our necks.

I scrambled onto the back of a hippokampoi and shouted, "Did Jude make it out?"

"She took the documents and left," Ares said.

Thank fates.

Ana and Cade climbed on behind me, and the hippokampoi shot through the water, speeding toward the portal. I turned around to watch the world devour itself. Mayhem flew alongside, silent and determined.

There was nothing but dust and destruction. As the golden light of the portal flashed, I realized that for the first time, I felt no pain in my wings.

~

On the other side of the golden portal, Kart-hadasht was dead silent. The portal back to Edinburgh glowed orange. We scrambled off the hippokampoi, and Mayhem zipped for the portal.

I turned back to them. "Thank you."

They each gave one of their burbly neighs, then swam off. I rushed through the orange portal with everyone else, spilling out into the darkened alley.

Tears stung my eyes, and my breath heaved. I sought Ana, grabbing her hands. "You saw her, right?"

Tears filled her eyes. "I did. I really did. It was Rowan."

"Your sister?" Cade asked.

The others looked on, eyes wide.

"It was her. I know it was her!" My mind raced, trying to remember every detail of what had just happened. "It was like she was under some kind of spell. The black oil that covered her had changed her eye color. Changed the signature of her magic."

"Then when it fell away, she looked like herself," Ana said. "Her eyes were blue again."

"She recognized me." I was sure of it. "As soon as the spell was lifted, she recognized me."

"It happened right when Nix finished removing the magic from the flame," Ana said.

"Oh, fates." It all clicked into place. "The Rebel Gods returned five years ago. When Rowan disappeared, they were the ones who abducted her. They used her magic to jumpstart their operations. That's why the magic in the stronghold felt strangely familiar." I spun toward Nix, who watched with wide eyes. "Can I see the rock? The one where you put the magic from the eternal flame."

"Sure." She handed it over.

As soon as I touched it, my jaw dropped. It was like holding Rowan's hand again. The scent of lilacs and the feel of a breeze hit me. Tears welled in my eyes.

"This is her magic," I said. "They took it from her and used it to fuel the stronghold."

Ana touched it and gasped, her gaze meeting mine. "It *is* hers."

"We have to save her," I said. "She didn't mean to do those things with the Rebel Gods. She's a captive, under their spell."

Cade wrapped an arm around my shoulders, supporting me when my legs turned weak.

Cass stepped forward and laid her hand on the rock. "All of the magic in here is pure. Good."

"They took her goodness and used it to create the stronghold," Ana said. "We have to get it back to her."

"We have to get *her* back."

We had to.

EPILOGUE

The next evening, after a long rest and healing, Jude and I walked through the forest toward the portal to Edinburgh. Mayhem, my new shadow, flew at our side. We were headed to the Whisky and Warlock for a victory celebration with the rest of the gang, though I was so worried about Rowan that my mind would be in two places.

But we had to formulate a game plan for the future, and it was just as easy to do so at the Whisky and Warlock. And as Jude said, sometimes you needed to focus on the good in life.

"You've done well, Bree," she said as we walked amongst the fairy lights.

"Thank you."

"Your magic is secure?"

I tested my wings, feeling no pain. "I think so. I did what you said—what the Valkyrie said. I looked before I leaped."

"What do you mean?"

"I was about to kill Rowan. Right before she was revealed, I was about to throw my dagger. She was down, weakened. I'd have killed her. But I waited. Something told me to wait."

"You listened to yourself, rather than just throwing yourself into the fray."

I nodded. "Well, it worked. I didn't kill my sister"—just the thought of it made bile rise in my throat—"and I think that's what earned me my wings. Now my magic comes when I call. I just have to practice using it to its fullest extent."

"You deserve that. And you're well on your way to succeeding at the academy. You've gone through trials that no trainee ever has to face."

"The biggest trial will be saving my sister. That wasn't her—they cursed her. She seemed different. Like she was overtaken by something. And she had new powers. Saving her is my priority now."

"As it should be. And we'll find a way. The documents that we stole will give us a good lead on the Rebel Gods. And we'll find out what they've done to your sister and how to break the curse. The Protectorate has contacts. I've called on some of them already. We'll see what they have to say."

"Thank you. Truly." Jude's help meant everything. She was my boss, not my mother. But that didn't keep me from feeling a similar warmth toward her.

"Of course," Jude said. "We're here for you. We're a team."

I smiled as we reached the portal in the clearing. We crossed through, stepping out onto the bustling city street in the Grassmarket. The sun shed a warm glow over the cobblestones, and the sound of bagpipes burst through the air, a busker on the High Street trying to make a buck. Or a pound, since we were in the UK.

The Whisky and Warlock was packed, as usual, with our crowd filling the little room where Sophie worked. The fire burned warmly in the hearth, and the beer taps gleamed in the light.

In the corner, Nix, Cass, and Del sat, along with Ares, Aidan, and Roarke. They'd said they'd come by to visit, and I was glad to see they'd showed up. Ana sat in the corner, joking around with Caro, Ali, and Haris, but I could see from her eyes and the set of her shoulders that she was thinking of Rowan.

Constantly. As I was.

I looked away from her, searching for Cade, who was on the other side of the room, near the bar. I gave him a nod before going over to my friends from Magic's Bend.

Mayhem headed straight for Sophie, probably to order a Ham-tini, which I doubted even existed.

I stopped at my friends' table. "Thank you guys again for all of your help. And for coming tonight."

Nix grinned. "Anytime. You helped us so much five years ago."

"When can we count on you visiting?" Cass said. "We're at P & P most Friday nights."

"The Friday night after I rescue my sister."

Del smiled, but her gaze was serious. "That's fair enough. If you need our help with her, just call. We may be able to do some tracking."

"Thank you, really." We shared a bit more small talk, but I could feel Cade's gaze burning into the back of my neck.

It warmed me all over, and eventually, I parted ways with my friends and approached Cade, who was turning from the bar. He held a pink martini glass in his hand that bubbled with glittery smoke.

"Developing new tastes?" I asked as I stopped in front of him.

"For you. Sophie's new special—the Valkyrie."

I smiled and took it. "You didn't tell her what I was, though, did you?"

I wanted to keep that on the down low. Bragging about my power wasn't my deal. And it was dangerous to let people know you were super powerful. Better to be underestimated.

"No. I just suggested the name." He smiled at me. "It suits you."

"Thanks." I took a sip, enjoying the tart taste.

"You were incredible in the stronghold," he said.

I smiled. "You weren't so bad yourself." I sobered a bit. "Thank you for always having my back."

I'd learned a lot about him these last couple days. His childhood had shocked me, but it only went to prove how strong and brave he was. He'd made his own way in the world, always choosing the side of right.

He was much more than just a super strong god wrapped in a hot package. So much more.

"I'll always have your back, Bree. I like you. And even if I didn't, I believe in you. You're going to accomplish great things. Important things that will make the world a better place. I want to be around for that."

"As long as one of those great things is saving my sister, then yes. I'm up for that." I'd do whatever it took.

"You'll save your sister. I believe in you. And tonight, we'll get started on planning exactly how we're going to do that."

Somehow, hearing him say it twice actually helped. I smiled up at him, my mind spinning with ways to find my sister and break the curse on her. I came up with nothing—but that didn't mean it would stay like that.

I'd find a way to save her. I had to. And with the help from my friends, my odds seemed even better.

THANK YOU FOR READING!

I hope you enjoyed *Pursuit of Magic*. Reviews are *so* helpful to authors. If you want to leave one, you can do so on Amazon or Goodreads.

Join my mailing list at www.linseyhall.com/subscribe to stay updated. You'll also get a free ebook copy of *Hidden Magic*. The story stars Cass, Del, and Nix, the FireSouls who help Bree in the final battle of this book.

EXCERPT OF HIDDEN MAGIC

Jungle, Southeast Asia
 Five years before the events in Ancient Magic

"How much are we being paid for this job again?" I glanced at the dudes filling the bar. It was a motley crowd of supernaturals, many of whom looked shifty as hell.

"Not nearly enough for one as dangerous as this." Del frowned at the man across the bar, who was giving her his best sexy face. There was a lot of eyebrow movement happening. "Is he having a seizure?"

"Looks like it." Nix grinned. "Though I gotta say, I wasn't expecting this. We're basically in a tree, for magic's sake. In the middle of the jungle! Where are all these dudes coming from?"

"According to my info, there's a mining operation near here. Though I'd say we're more *under* a tree than *in* a tree."

"I'm with Cass," Del said. "Under, not in."

"Fair enough," Nix said.

We were deep in Southeast Asia, in a bar that had long ago been reclaimed by the jungle. A massive fig tree had grown over and around the ancient building, its huge roots strangling the stone walls. It was straight out of a fairy tale.

Monks had once lived here, but a few supernaturals of indeterminate species had gotten ahold of it and turned it into a watering hole for the local supernaturals. We were meeting our contact here, but he was late.

"Hey, pretty lady." A smarmy voice sounded from my left. "What are you?"

I turned to face the guy who was giving me the up and down, his gaze roving from my tank top to my shorts. He wasn't Clarence, our local contact. And if he meant "what kind of supernatural are you?" I sure as hell wouldn't be answering. That could get me killed.

"Not interested is what I am," I said.

"Aww, that's no way to treat a guy." He grabbed my hip, rubbed his thumb up and down.

I smacked his hand away, tempted to throat-punch him. It was my favorite move, but I didn't want to start a fight before Clarence got here. Didn't want to piss off our boss.

The man raised his hands. "Hey, hey. No need to get feisty. You three sisters?"

I glanced at Nix and Del, at their dark hair that was so different from my red. We were all about twenty, but we looked nothing alike. And while we might call ourselves sisters—*deirfiúr* in our native Irish—this idiot didn't know that.

"Go away." I had no patience for dirt bags who touched me without asking. "Run along and flirt with your hand, because that's all the action you'll be getting tonight."

His face turned a mottled red, and he raised a fist. His magic welled, the scent of rotten fruit overwhelming.

He thought he was going to smack me? Or use his magic against me?

Ha.

I lashed out, punching him in the throat. His eyes bulged and he gagged. I kneed him in the crotch, grinning when he keeled over.

"Hey!" A burly man with a beard lunged for us, his buddy beside him following. "That's no way—"

"To treat a guy?" I finished for him as I kicked out at him. My tall, heavy boots collided with his chest, sending him flying backward. I never used my magic—didn't want to go to jail and didn't want to blow things up—but I sure as hell could fight.

His friend raised his hand and sent a blast of wind at us. It threw me backward, sending me skidding across the floor.

By the time I'd scrambled to my feet, a brawl had broken out in the bar. Fists flew left and right, with a bit of magic thrown in. Nothing bad enough to ruin the bar, like jets of flame, because no one wanted to destroy the only watering hole for a hundred miles, but enough that it lit up the air with varying magical signatures.

Nix conjured a baseball bat and swung it at a burly guy who charged her, while Del teleported behind a horned demon and smashed a chair over his head. I'd always been jealous of Del's ability to sneak up on people like that.

All in all, it was turning into a good evening. A fight between supernaturals was fun.

"Enough!" the bartender bellowed. "Or no more beer!"

The patrons quieted immediately. Fights might be fun, but they weren't worth losing beer over.

I glared at the jerk who'd started it. There was no way I'd take the blame, even though I'd thrown the first punch. He should have known better.

The bartender gave me a look and I shrugged, hiking a thumb at the jerk who'd touched me. "He shoulda kept his hands to himself."

"Fair enough," the bartender said.

I nodded and turned to find Nix and Del. They'd grabbed our

beers and were putting them on a table in the corner. I went to join them.

We were a team. Sisters by choice, ever since we'd woken in a field at fifteen with no memories other than those that said we were FireSouls on the run from someone who had hurt us. Who was hunting us.

Our biggest goal, even bigger than getting out from under our current boss's thumb, was to save enough money to buy conceal-ment charms that would hide us from the monster who hunted us. He was just a shadowy memory, but it was enough to keep us running.

"Where is Clarence, anyway?" I pulled my damp tank top away from my sweaty skin. The jungle was damned hot. We couldn't break into the temple until Clarence gave us the infor-mation we needed to get past the guard at the front. And we didn't need to spend too much longer in this bar.

Del glanced at her watch, her blue eyes flashing with annoy-ance. "He's twenty minutes late. Old Man Bastard said he should be here at eight."

Old Man Bastard—OMB for short—was our boss. His name said it all. Del, Nix, and I were FireSouls, the most despised species of supernatural because we could steal other magical being's powers if we killed them. We'd never done that, of course, but OMB didn't care. He'd figured out our secret when we were too young to hide it effectively and had been blackmailing us to work for him ever since.

It'd been four years of finding and stealing treasure on his behalf. Treasure hunting was our other talent, a gift from the dragon with whom legend said we shared a soul. No one had seen a dragon in centuries, so I wasn't sure if the legend was even true, but dragons were covetous, so it made sense they had a knack for finding treasure.

"What are we after again?" Nix asked.

"A pair of obsidian daggers," Del said. "Nice ones."

"And how much is this job worth?" Nix repeated my earlier question. Money was always on our minds. It was our only chance at buying our freedom, but OMB didn't pay us enough for it to be feasible anytime soon. We kept meticulous track of our earnings and saved like misers anyway.

"A thousand each."

"Damn, that's pathetic." I slouched back in my chair and stared up at the ceiling, too bummed about our crappy pay to even be impressed by the stonework and vines above my head.

"Hey, pretty ladies." The oily voice made my skin crawl. We just couldn't get a break in here. I looked up to see Clarence, our contact.

Clarence was a tall man, slender as a vine, and had the slicked back hair and pencil-thin mustache of a 1940s movie star. Unfortunately, it didn't work on him. Probably because his stare was like a lizard's. He was more Gomez Addams than Clark Gable. I'd bet anything that he liked working for OMB.

"Hey, Clarence," I said. "Pull up a seat and tell us how to get into the temple."

Clarence slid into a chair, his movement eerily snakelike. I shivered and scooted my chair away, bumping into Del. The scent of her magic flared, a clean hit of fresh laundry, as she no doubt suppressed her instinct to transport away from Clarence. If I had her gift of teleportation, I'd have to repress it as well.

"How about a drink first?" Clarence said.

Del growled, but Nix interjected, her voice almost nice. She had the most self control out of the three of us. "No can do, Clarence. You know... Mr. Oribis"—her voice tripped on the name, probably because she wanted to call him OMB—"wants the daggers soon. Maybe next time, though."

"Next time." Clarence shook his head like he didn't believe her. He might be a snake, but he was a clever one. His chest puffed up a bit. "You know I'm the only one who knows how to get into the temple. How to get into any of the places in this jungle."

"And we're so grateful you're meeting with us. Mr. Oribis is so grateful." Nix dug into her pocket and pulled out the crumpled envelope that contained Clarence's pay. We'd counted it and found—unsurprisingly—that it was more than ours combined, even though all he had to do was chat with us for two minutes. I'd wanted to scream when I'd seen it.

Clarence's gaze snapped to the money. "All right, all right."

Apparently his need to be flattered went out the window when cash was in front of his face. Couldn't blame him, though. I was the same way.

"So, what are we up against?" I asked.

The temple containing the daggers had been built by supernaturals over a thousand years ago. Like other temples of its kind, it was magically protected. Clarence's intel would save us a ton of time and damage to the temple if we could get around the enchantments rather than breaking through them.

"Dvarapala. A big one."

"A gatekeeper?" I'd seen one of the giant, stone monster statues at another temple before.

"Yep." He nodded slowly. "Impossible to get through. The temple's as big as the Titanic—hidden from humans, of course—but no one's been inside in centuries, they say."

Hidden from humans was a given. They had no idea supernaturals existed, and we wanted to keep it that way.

"So how'd you figure out the way in?" Del asked. "And why *haven't* you gone in? Bet there's lots of stuff you could fence in there. Temples are usually full of treasure."

"A bit of pertinent research told me how to get in. And I'd rather sell the entrance information and save my hide. It won't be easy to get past the booby traps in there."

Hide? Snakeskin, more like. Though he had a point. I didn't think he'd last long trying to get through a temple on his own.

"So? Spill it," I said, anxious to get going.

He leaned in, and the overpowering scent of cologne and sweat hit me. I grimaced, held my breath, then leaned forward to hear his whispers.

~

As soon as Clarence walked away, the communications charms around my neck vibrated. I jumped, then groaned. Only one person had access to this charm.

I shoved the small package Clarence had given me into my short's pocket and pressed my fingertips to the comms charm, igniting its magic.

"Hello, Mr. Oribis." I swallowed my bile at having to be polite.

"Girls," he grumbled.

Nix made a gagging face. We hated when he called us girls.

"Change of plans. You need to go to the temple tonight."

"What? But it's dark. We're going tomorrow." He never changed the plans on us. This was weird.

"I need the daggers sooner. Go tonight."

My mind raced. "The jungle is more dangerous in the dark. We'll do it if you pay us more."

"Twice the usual," Del said.

A tinny laugh echoed from the charm. "Pay *you* more? You're lucky I pay you at all."

I gritted my teeth and said, "But we've been working for you for four years without a raise."

"And you'll be working for me for four more years. And four after that. And four after that." Annoyance lurked in his tone. So did his low opinion of us.

Del's and Nix's brows crinkled in distress. We'd always suspected that OMB wasn't planning to let us buy our freedom, but he'd dangled that carrot in front of us. What he'd just said made that seem like a big fat lie, though. One we could add to the many others he'd told us.

An urge to rebel, to stand up to the bully who controlled our lives, seethed in my chest.

"No," I said. "You treat us like crap, and I'm sick of it. Pay us fairly."

"I treat you like *crap*, as you so eloquently put it, because that is exactly what you are. *FireSouls*." He spit the last word, imbuing it with so much venom I thought it might poison me.

I flinched, frantically glancing around to see if anyone in the bar had heard what he'd called us. Fortunately, they were all distracted. That didn't stop my heart from thundering in my ears as rage replaced the fear. I opened my mouth to shout at him, but snapped it shut. I was too afraid of pissing him off.

"Get it by dawn," he barked. "Or I'm turning one of you in to the Order of the Magica. Prison will be the least of your worries. They might just execute you."

I gasped. "You wouldn't." Our government hunted and imprisoned—or destroyed—FireSouls.

"Oh, I would. And I'd enjoy it. The three of you have been more trouble than you're worth. You're getting cocky, thinking you have a say in things like this. Get the daggers by dawn, or one of you ends up in the hands of the Order."

My skin chilled, and the floor felt like it had dropped out from under me. He was serious.

"Fine." I bit off the end of the word, barely keeping my voice from shaking. "We'll do it tonight. Del will transport them to you as soon as we have them."

"Excellent." Satisfaction rang in his tone, and my skin crawled. "Don't disappoint me, or you know what will happen."

The magic in the charm died. He'd broken the connection.

I collapsed back against the chair. In times like these, I wished I had it in me to kill. Sure, I offed demons when they came at me on our jobs, but that was easy because they didn't actually die. Killing their earthly bodies just sent them back to their hell.

But I couldn't kill another supernatural. Not even OMB. It might get us out of this lifetime of servitude, but I didn't have it in me. And what if I failed? I was too afraid of his rage—and the consequences—if I didn't succeed.

"Shit, shit, shit." Nix's green eyes were stark in her pale face. "He means it."

"Yeah." Del's voice shook. "We need to get those daggers."

"Now," I said.

"I wish I could just conjure a forgery," Nix said. "I really don't want to go out into the jungle tonight. Getting past the Dvarapala in the dark will suck."

Nix was a conjurer, able to create almost anything using just her magic. Massive or complex things, like airplanes or guns, were outside of her ability, but a couple of daggers wouldn't be hard.

Trouble was, they were a magical artifact, enchanted with the ability to return to whoever had thrown them. Like boomerangs. Though Nix could conjure the daggers, we couldn't enchant them.

"We need to go. We only have six hours until dawn." I grabbed my short swords from the table and stood, shoving them into the holsters strapped to my back.

A hush descended over the crowded bar.

I stiffened, but the sound of the staticky TV in the corner made me relax. They weren't interested in me. Just the news, which was probably being routed through a dozen techno-witches to get this far into the jungle.

The grave voice of the female reporter echoed through the quiet bar. "The FireSoul was apprehended outside of his apartment in Magic's Bend, Oregon. He is currently in the custody of the Order of the Magica, and his trial is scheduled for tomorrow morning. My sources report that execution is possible."

I stifled a crazed laugh. Perfect timing. Just what we needed to hear after OMB's threat. A reminder of what would happen if he turned us into the Order of the Magica. The hush that had descended over the previously rowdy crowd—the kind of hush you get at the scene of a big accident—indicated what an interesting freaking topic this was. FireSouls were the bogeymen. *I* was the bogeyman, even though I didn't use my powers. But as long as no one found out, we were safe.

My gaze darted to Del and Nix. They nodded toward the door. It was definitely time to go.

As the newscaster turned her report toward something more boring and the crowd got rowdy again, we threaded our way between the tiny tables and chairs.

I shoved the heavy wooden door open and sucked in a breath of sticky jungle air, relieved to be out of the bar. Night creatures screeched, and moonlight filtered through the trees above. The jungle would be a nice place if it weren't full of things that wanted to kill us.

"We're never escaping him, are we?" Nix said softly.

"We will." Somehow. Someday. "Let's just deal with this for now."

We found our motorcycles, which were parked in the lot with a dozen other identical ones. They were hulking beasts with massive, all-terrain tires meant for the jungle floor. We'd done a lot of work in Southeast Asia this year, and these were our favored forms of transportation in this part of the world.

Del could transport us, but it was better if she saved her power. It wasn't infinite, though it did regenerate. But we'd learned a long time ago to save Del's power for our escape. Nothing worse than being trapped in a temple with pissed off guardians and a few tripped booby traps.

We'd scouted out the location of the temple earlier that day, so we knew where to go.

I swung my leg over Secretariat—I liked to name my vehicles

—and kicked the clutch. The engine roared to life. Nix and Del followed, and we peeled out of the lot, leaving the dingy yellow light of the bar behind.

Our headlights illuminated the dirt road as we sped through the night. Huge fig trees dotted the path on either side, their twisted trunks and roots forming an eerie corridor. Elephant-ear sized leaves swayed in the wind, a dark emerald that gleamed in the light.

Jungle animals howled, and enormous lightning bugs flitted along the path. They were too big to be regular bugs, so they were most likely some kind of fairy, but I wasn't going to stop to investigate. There were dangerous creatures in the jungle at night —one of the reasons we hadn't wanted to go now—and in our world, fairies could be considered dangerous.

Especially if you called them lightning bugs.

A roar sounded in the distance, echoing through the jungle and making the leaves rustle on either side as small animals scurried for safety.

The roar came again, only closer.

Then another, and another.

"Oh shit," I muttered. This was bad.

~~~

Join my mailing list at www.linseyhall.com/subscribe to get a free ebook copy of *Hidden Magic.* No spam and you can leave anytime!

AUTHOR'S NOTE

Thanks for reading *Pursuit of Magic!* The author's note is where I normally talk about the history and mythology in the book, and boy, was *Pursuit of Magic* full of it. I've wanted to write a book featuring Viking mythology for ages and this was so much fun. The addition of Phoenician history was icing on the cake, as the excavation of a Phoenician shipwreck was one of my favorite experiences as an archaeologist.

To start—Veronica and Doug are real archaeologists who make 3D models of archaeological sites and artifacts. They use cameras and drones, as well as some fancy software, and were kind enough to agree to appear in *Pursuit of Magic.* Click here to check out some of their 3D models of artifacts on their Interactive Heritage website. If you check back regularly, there will be more cool stuff to see. The goal of their work is to make history and archaeology more accessible to people all over the world, and I think they do an amazing job.

Next, the Cave of Seers was based on Smoo Cave, which is a sea cave located on the north coast of Scotland. Give it a google and check out the pictures—they are amazing. The cave goes back deep into the cliff and you could take a little boat on the underground river. The most interesting part of the cave, however, is the fact that Vikings really did use it as a stopping point on their journeys to raid and colonize the British Isles. They often repaired their boats in the cave, and Viking tools and ship pieces have been found there.

When the Viking ship built itself using magic, I was a bit vague with the terms. I didn't want to overload the story with technical stuff that would slow it down. However, I was a nautical archaeologist before I was a writer, and this was one of my favorite parts. Vikings were some of the greatest sea-farers in history. Their ships were open vessels featuring lapstrake construction—meaning that the side planks overlapped each other. They were beautiful, amazing ships—but they were basically giant, open rowboats. There was no interior cabin where a Viking sailor could go to sleep or get out of the weather—and they sailed these boats across the North Atlantic! That blows my mind every time I think about it.

The Norse realm that Bree enters is based on mythology, which for the Vikings was an oral history recorded by poets during the Viking age. The most famous of these was Snorri Sturluson, who I believe I've mentioned in other books. He lived in Iceland in the 12th and 13th centuries AD and recorded much of their history. I borrowed a bit from mythology and history and also put my own spin on it.

Yggdrasil is indeed called the World Tree and the nine realms of the Norse gods are held within the tree's roots and branches. There's a bit of scholarly disagreement about which of the realms were truly part of the nine. Muspell, the land of the Fire Giants, may or may not have been officially included—but I liked it so much that I made it a realm for Bree to explore. The Valkyrie did not have their own realm—they are most commonly associated with living at Valhalla in Asgard—but I gave them their own realm because I thought they deserved it.

The Valkyrie have an interesting history in how they have

been depicted throughout time. Depending upon which source you read, they are fierce warriors or lovely maidens who served mead in Valhalla, waiting upon the deceased warriors who partied the night away as they waited for Ragnarok, the end of the world and the greatest battle of all time. You may have an inkling of what version I prefer— the fierce warrior version! Those dudes can get their own mead.

The Valkyrie's most famous job was to choose the worthy from the slain and lead them to Valhalla, Odin's amazing hall where the warriors would drink mead with Odin and wait for Ragnarok. One of the oldest versions of this story was particularly fascinating. It comes from the *Darraðarljóð*, a poem contained within *Njal's Saga*, which was written in Iceland in the 13th century AD. It regards events that occurred between 960 and 1020 AD (most sagas were written in Iceland, a Viking colony).

The saga tells of the Valkyrie taking an active role in choosing those who would die and go to Valhalla. They did not roam the fields after the battle was over, choosing from the already slain. Instead, they selected the most powerful and worthy fighters before the battle ever started. They then used magic and whatever means they had at their disposal to insure that those men died on the battlefield and could be taken to Valhalla, where they would train and celebrate until Ragnarok arrived. Specifically, the *Darraðarljóð* poem tells of 12 Valkyrie weaving on grisly looms prior to the Battle of Clontarf (Ireland, April 23rd, 1014 AD). The looms used intestines for threads and severed heads for loom weights. Swords and arrows acted as beaters, the part of the loom that pushes the weaving firmly into place. I'm not saying that the Valkyrie in my story did this (it's a bit *too* grisly), but they are warriors in their own right. And the men served themselves mead :-).

The three fates who Bree encountered at the world tree are based on the Norns, popular figures from Norse mythology. Their names and the meanings of their names were derived from historical sources. The well that they consulted for Bree is called the Well of Urd and it sits beneath Yggdrasil. In some sources, the Norns are said to live within the well, but I gave them a long-house, the traditional dwelling of the Vikings.

The Fire Giants and dark elves are part of Norse mythology, as is Ratatoskr, the giant gossipy squirrel. Ratatoskr is one of my favorite mythological figures and was possibly the most fun character I've ever written. He is said to carry slanderous gossip between the serpent at the bottom of the tree, named Níðhöggr, and the eagle at the top. The eagle is nameless, but a hawk named Veðrfölnir sits on the eagle's head, between his eyes. I omitted the hawk for clarity's sake. Ratatoskr delights in his job of provoking the eagle and the serpent, so you can see why he would be horrified if they suddenly became friends.

Back at the Protectorate castle, Florian used a selection of insults to refer to Potts, the day librarian. They are real historic insults. Initially, I asked my Facebook group, the FireSouls (we'd love you to join!), to vote on their favorite insult. Saddle-goose won, but they were all so good that I had to include them. Since they are fun, here are some definitions. A saddle-goose is someone who is stupid enough to try to saddle a goose, which is a fundamentally useless endeavor since you can't ride a goose. Though this term was most popular in the 19th century, it could be as old as the 14th. Scobberlotcher means someone who doesn't work hard, and is likely derived from *scopperloit*, the old English word for vacation. Lubberwort is a 16th century word for a plant that was thought to cause stupidity or sluggishness, and it was eventually used to refer to people. Finally, a fopdoodle is a foolish person.

Now, onto the Phoenicians and Kart-hadasht. The Phoenicians were a seafaring culture that sailed the Mediterranean between 1500 BC and 300 BC. They originated in the area that now contains Syria, Palestine, Lebanon, Israel, and part of Turkey, but they spread their settlements and culture as far as the western Mediterranean. Carthage, in Tunisia, was their most notable colony. I chose the Phoenicians for a number of reasons, one of which was that I've been fond of them since excavating a Phoenician shipwreck near Cartagena, Spain.

Some of the most interesting things that we found on the site (which was 70 feet underwater near the reef that destroyed the ship) were elephant tusks carved with Phoenician writing. I don't approve of elephant hunting or ivory collecting, but these were thousands of years old and therefore outside of the modern day ivory trade (which is terrible). There were no elephants in *Pursuit of Magic*, but Bree did encounter some minotaur-like monsters that had tusks carved with writing. They were inspired by the shipwreck, which is called the Bajo de la Campana wreck if you'd like to give it a google and learn more. The photos are amazing.

Kart-hadasht is the original name of Carthage, but in *Pursuit of Magic*, it is an invented Phoenician city on the coast of Tunisia. Normally, I like to use real archaeological sites in my books, but the Phoenicians did such a fabulous job of choosing sites for their cities that people never left, even after thousands of years. Therefor, the ancient Phoenician ruins at places like Carthage, Byblos, Tyre, and Sidon are in pretty rough shape. Thousands of years will do that to a city.

Eternal flames were an element of Phoenician temples, and Carthage likely contained a Temple of Melqart. Melqart was a Phoenician god associated with the sea (are you noticing a trend here?), colonization, and commercial trade. The Phoenician letters in the mosaic pool that surrounded the eternal flame were taken from real Phoenician letters that mean *door* and *window*, and the Phoenicians alphabet is the oldest verified alphabet. It was a no-brainer to use this as one of the challenges for Bree.

Finally, the three Rebel Gods who attack Bree and her friends at the Temple of Melquart were based on real gods. The huge man surrounded by flurries of snow was Chernobog, a Slavic deity from the 12th century AD. Not much is known about Chernobog, and I imagine that he would want more power because of this.

The god with golden horns was Cocidius, a Romano-Celtic war god from the area around Hadrian's wall, which separates England and Scotland. During this period (around 122 AD when the wall was built), the Romans were attempting to conquer Britain, which was full of Celts and Picts. Their religions melded, as they often can, and Cocidius was worshipped by both Romans and Celtic Britons. He was primarily worshipped by warriors and the lower classes, and I imagine he has a bit of a chip on his shoulder because of this.

The greek looking goddess who dripped blood from her skin was Elis, the Greek goddess of chaos, who loved battles and war. The blood was my addition. She is the daughter of Zeus and Hera, but because of her unpleasant disposition, she was generally snubbed by the other gods and mankind as well. She is an excellent candidate for an angry and vengeful Rebel God.

Last, the city in Tunisia where Bree, Cade, and Ana find Doug and Veronica is based on Tataouine, a real city in Tunisia. It is an amazing place and I tried to describe it as accurately as possible, but it's so unusual that it might be hard to picture. I highly recommend you google it. I bet you'll be as impressed as I was. And if the name Tataouine sounds familiar, that's because this place inspired Tatooine in the Star Wars films.

Well, I think that's it for the history and mythology in *Pursuit of Magic*. This one was extra fun to write because of all the mythology, and I hope you enjoyed it and will come back for more of Bree, Ana, and Cade!

ACKNOWLEDGMENTS

Thank you, Ben, for everything. There would be no books without you.

Thank you to Lindsey Loucks and Jena O'Connor for your excellent editing. The book is immensely better because of you! And thank you Eleonora, for your keen eye in spotting errors.

Thank you to Orina Kafe for the beautiful cover art. Thank you to Collette Markwardt for allowing me to borrow the Pugs of Destruction, who are real dogs named Chaos, Havoc, and Ruckus. They were all adopted from rescue agencies.

GLOSSARY

Alpha Council - There are two governments that enforce law for supernaturals—the Alpha Council and the Order of the Magica. The Alpha Council governs all shifters. They work cooperatively with the Alpha Council when necessary—for example, when capturing FireSouls.

Blood Sorcerer - A type of Magica who can create magic using blood.

Dark Magic - The kind that is meant to harm. It's not necessarily bad, but it often is.

Demons - Often employed to do evil. They live in various hells but can be released upon the earth if you know how to get to them and then get them out. If they are killed on Earth, they are sent back to their hell.

Dragon Sense - A FireSoul's ability to find treasure. It is an internal sense that pulls them toward what they seek. It is easiest to find gold, but they can find anything or anyone that is valued by someone.

Djinn - Possesses invisibility and the ability to possess others for brief periods of time.

Earthwalking Gods - Reincarnates of the ancient gods who

can walk upon the earth. They are mortal but with all the power of that god.

Eclektica - A jack-of-all-trades who deals in spells.

Enchanted Artifacts – Artifacts can be imbued with magic that lasts after the death of the person who put the magic into the artifact (unlike a spell that has not been put into an artifact—these spells disappear after the Magica's death). But magic is not stable. After a period of time—hundreds or thousands of years depending on the circumstance—the magic will degrade. Eventually, it can go bad and cause many problems.

Fire Mage – A mage who can control fire.

FireSoul - A very rare type of Magica who shares a piece of the dragon's soul. They can locate treasure and steal the gifts (powers) of other supernaturals. With practice, they can manipulate the gifts they steal, becoming the strongest of that gift. They are despised and feared. If they are caught, they are thrown in the Prison of Magical Deviants.

The Great Peace - The most powerful piece of magic ever created. It hides magic from the eyes of humans.

Magica - Any supernatural who has the power to create magic —witches, sorcerers, mages. All are governed by the Order of the Magica.

Order of the Magica - There are two governments that enforce law for supernaturals—the Alpha Council and the Order of the Magica. The Order of the Magica govern all Magica. They work cooperatively with the Alpha Council when necessary—for example, when capturing FireSouls.

Seeker - A type of supernatural who can find things. FireSouls often pass off their dragon sense as Seeker power.

Seklie - Sea creatures lived off the coasts of Ireland and Scotland. They are seals who can also become human and draw their magic from the sea.

Shifter - A supernatural who can turn into an animal. All are governed by the Alpha Council.

Transporter - A type of supernatural who can travel anywhere. Their power is limited and must regenerate after each use.

Undercover Protectorate - A secret organization dedicated to protecting supernaturals and solving the crimes that no one else will.

Vampire - Blood drinking supernaturals with great strength and speed who live in a separate realm.

ABOUT LINSEY

Before becoming a writer, Linsey Hall was a nautical archaeologist who studied shipwrecks from Hawaii and the Yukon to the UK and the Mediterranean. She credits fantasy and historical romances with her love of history and her career as an archaeologist. After a decade of tromping around the globe in search of old bits of stuff that people left lying about, she settled down and started penning her own romance novels. Her Dragon's Gift series draws upon her love of history and the paranormal elements that she can't help but include.

COPYRIGHT